D0140071

THE SCIENCE OF PAUL

DEC - - 2018

PRAISE FOR

THE SCIENCE OF PAUL

by Aaron Philip Clark

"A finely-drawn character study of a man battling fate to escape the inevitable gravity of a life of crime. Reminiscent of the existential crime novels of Jean-Patrick Manchette. That we care so much about Paul is testament to Aaron Philip Clark's skill."

—Eric Beetner, author of **ONE TOO MANY BLOWS TO THE HEAD** and **BORROWED TROUBLE**

"Aaron Philip Clark's THE SCIENCE OF PAUL has all the makings of a modern noir classic. Noir in its purest form always reads like a punch to the gut and THE SCIENCE OF PAUL delivers that kind of blow right from page one. 'No apologies, no regrets' should be this novel's motto."

—Gar Anthony Haywood, author of **CEMETERY ROAD**

"The eponymous protagonist of Aaron Clarke's scorching, gripping THE SCIENCE OF PAUL is an ex-con, a booze hound, a haunted drifter. Deep in the heart of America's south, which seems only just north of hell, he emotionlessly buries his grandfather and, with a beautiful woman in tow, drives off at full speed, slap-bang into the classic noir paradigm. This is a car wreck well worth risking your neck to see."

—Paul D. Brazill, **LAST YEAR'S MAN**

"With the relentless moth-to-flame inevitability of classic noir, Aaron Philip Clark's angry ex-con finds trouble on Philadelphia's mean streets. Vivid characterization and a sharp eye for the fault lines in American society drive this impressive debut."

—Roger Smith, author of **WAKE UP DEAD** and **MIXED BLOOD**

"T.S. Eliot referred to it as tradition and individual talent, the manner in which new work at once honors, builds upon, and questions what has come before. Chester Himes, Richard Wright, James Baldwin—Aaron Philip Clark has been paying attention."

—James Sallis, author of **CYPRESS GROVE** and **CHESTER HIMES: A LIFE**

THE
SCIENCE

OF PAUL

WILLIAMSBURG REGIONAL LIBRARY
7770 CROAKER ROAD
WILLIAMSBURG, VA 23188

A NOVEL OF CRIME

AARON PHILIP CLARK

SHOTGUN
HONEY

The Science of Paul: A Novel of Crime
Text copyright © 2011, 2018 Aaron Philip Clark

All rights reserved. This book or any portion thereof may not be reproduced or used in any manner whatsoever without the express written permission of the publisher except for the use of brief quotations in a book review.

This book is a work of fiction. Names, characters, places, and incidents either are products of the author's imagination or are used fictitiously. Any resemblance to actual persons, living or dead, events, or locales is entirely coincidental.

Published by Shotgun Honey, an imprint of Down & Out Books

Shotgun Honey
PO Box 75272
Charleston, WV 25375
www.ShotgunHoney.com

Down & Out Books
3959 Van Dyke Rd, Ste. 265
Lutz, FL 33558
www.DownAndOutBooks.com

Cover Design by Bad Fido.

First Printing 2018

ISBN-10: 1-948235-00-5
ISBN-13: 978-1-948235-00-6

For my family

SCIENCE OF PAUL
a novel of crime

CHAPTER ONE

MY GRANDFATHER DIED in his one-bedroom house on thirteen acres in rural North Carolina. His friend and one-time lover, Margaret, found him. Margaret used to bring him home-cooked meals twice a week and had cleaned his house on the third of every month. Part of me feels guilty for not inviting her to his burial, but I needed to put him in the ground myself. Margaret would have demanded a traditional service. She would have cried, hollered, moaned and clung to the body in some dramatic portrayal of a grief-stricken lover, something my grandfather wouldn't have wanted. He always said Southern funerals were like auditions for chitlin circuit plays. They were contests to see who could holler the loudest and faint the hardest. He hated funerals—I hate funerals.

I rest my arm on the splintered handle of the shovel. Sweat beads down my shoulder, to my wrist, then curls around my finger and harbors under the nail before dripping into the dirt. Watching as the sweat mixes with the red clay, I wonder if the earth mourns men when they die. Does it know when a living creature's time has come to an end? Does the earth welcome the deceased home? Or does it go right to work, heedlessly breaking down the minutia of cells in the meat and bone?

The casket is thin pine. The hinges have been taken from a pantry door, and the wood is already showing signs of critter infestation. It was all I could afford. My grandfather was meek; he wouldn't care, but nobody should be buried like this—just a hair above how a family might bury their long-time pet. I ponder throwing in a few of his things. Perhaps a pair of dress loafers, his bow tie collection, his Bible, photos of his beloved candy apple red Austin-Healey Sprite. I know what my grandfather would say if he could: shoes are no good where he's going, the Austin-Healey is a rust bucket, and I should keep the Bible for myself.

I glance up at Tammy, who is sitting on the trunk of her white 1984 Cadillac Seville. Her feet are comfortably propped on the bumper and her yellow sundress is blowing in the sweltering breeze. She's exotic, breathtaking: full lips, cinnamon eyes intensified by halos of green, all compliment her bronzed skin. Years of college track have blessed her with toned calves and a flat stomach. Watching her is like watching some endangered species of butterfly or hummingbird, a kind of graceful exquisiteness. It's always special, because I know our time together is coming to a close. Tammy is what men grow weak and rubbery in the knees for—she's proof of God's existence and even if she lives to be ninety, I doubt her beauty will ever fade. But every time I look at her, I can't help but ask myself, *Why the hell is she with me*?

"You about ready?" she asks.

I lay the shovel on the ground and take a folded piece of

notebook paper from my back pocket. The eulogy is a few lines with words jotted in blue ink. My grandfather deserves a million more words, but lately my words have been failing.

I whisper the eulogy so Tammy cannot hear. She has a way of making moments like this saccharine sweet, and everything is too damn precious for words.

I finish reading. She smiles, wiping the salty sheen from her arms with a damp cloth. My grandfather always said there was only one way out of life. How easy things would be if I were in that pine casket instead of him. He loved life. I can take it or leave it. Still, in the face of my despair I can't deny the beauty that is the land. I had forgotten how serene it is: the cicadas call, the high cotton communes with the wind, and the thick aroma of earth accents its beauty like a woman swathed in a majestic perfume. This is where I belong. I was made here. My history is in the soil. My grandfather told me stories of his life here. He and his drinking buddies sitting around a card table, dominoes scattered, and a whiskey bottle shy of the last round. Cigarette smoke so thick it looks like lifting fog. They told of scarred-up backs, crooked noses, and bruised pride for looking at blue eyes for too long, for talking back to white men, for being uppity, for having a stride and straight back worthy of kings. But fighting tooth and nail didn't stop them from loving their home, and when it came time for that last round, they drank to the South like it were a fallen comrade, deceased but not forgotten; eulogizing its hope and anguish, paying their respects in jeers and fondness. It was all they knew, and somewhere between the tears, blood, and bodies that fell, they claimed it as their own.

I close my eyes and imagine … I could be content here, on the land, alone, quiet so I can think, so things can finally make sense. I could plant, harvest, and fish. I could grow tobacco, learn to cure it, sell it at the markets, live like my grandfather did—alone and at peace.

"Paul?"

I open my eyes and Tammy tosses me a bottle of water. I crack the seal and take it down fast.

"You should take a break or something," she says, getting back into the Caddy. She turns on the air-conditioning. Tammy is always concerned about my well-being, but today, just today, I wish she would leave me be. I go back to filling the grave, ignoring her advice.

I'm no stranger to the heat. Growing up I worked the farm with my grandfather. From sun up to sundown, we plowed brush, trimmed hedges, and tended to his vegetable garden. At the end of the day we would sit under the dogwood and rest. God, how he loved his dogwood, so I thought it only fitting to bury him beside its roots.

The grave is nearly filled when Tammy gets out of the car to check on my progress.

"Should I put some flowers on top?" she asks. Before I can answer, she plucks a cluster of dandelions and ties them together with stem and root.

"These are nice," she says. She walks over and gently places them on the grave. She takes two steps back to admire her work. "See, nature's headstone. So it doesn't just look like a mound of dirt."

"It is a mound of dirt," I say. "It's a grave."

"You know what I mean."

I tidy up my work, flattening the grave with the back of the shovel. I knock the excess dirt off and wrap the tool in a black trash bag.

"Pop the trunk, will you?" I ask.

The trunk bounces open and I lay the shovel near the bags of my grandfather's belongings. I get into the Caddy and Tammy turns the ignition. After two blasts of exhaust, the Caddy roars to life. Every time the engine turns over, I'm reminded of the thick black residue that's collected around the tailpipe and how I've been meaning to clean it.

We roll down the long dirt driveway. I look back toward my grandfather's farm and say a silent farewell. Tammy accelerates over a pothole and the peaceful valediction is short-lived.

"Watch it," I say, as she struggles to maneuver over the massive craters and ditches, "you'll knock it out of line."

"I know," she says. "This road is a headache."

"Do you know how to get back to Interstate 40?" I ask.

"Yes, but I want to stop for sandwiches. You're not hungry?"

"I can eat," I say.

Tammy pulls onto the main stretch, and I watch as the speedometer reaches 60 miles per hour and then teeters back to 55. The Cadillac breathes three hundred horses between white lines. The engine is strong. Tammy had it rebuilt after her father passed away—it has only thirty thousand miles on it. It was around that time she discovered her passion for road trips. She thought getting out of the city would help strengthen our relationship—us, the open road, and sandwiches. She picked rustic places to drive to, like the Pennsylvania hill country and the Poconos. She soon learned that the Caddy didn't do well with highlands. It was too heavy and hard to steer when coasting down hills, and we could smell burning oil when climbing steep inclines.

We drive about twenty minutes down the road when Tammy pulls into the parking lot of a chain grocery and parks the Caddy about ten spaces down from the store.

"I'll be right back," she says.

Tammy grabs her purse and leaves the key in the ignition.

I tune the radio, trying to find anything besides gospel and country. A pick-up truck pulls into the spot next to the Caddy. A heavy-set man, white, shirtless, and sunburnt gets out. He looks at me; his head cocked sideways, spits, mumbles something, and then heads into the store. I notice a small boy moving about in the truck. He's about nine, his face splattered with freckles. The red blotches are so densely clustered, they look like they've been painted on. He looks at me from the passenger's seat and then crawls into the driver's seat and starts jerking the wheel from side to side. Making motor sounds with his mouth and the occasional *honk, honk*, he checks over his shoulder anticipating the shirtless man's return.

I notice on the dented truck gate a faded white sticker with red words that read THE SOUTH WILL RISE AGAIN. Irritated and hungry, I watch as the boy jerks the wheel until it finally locks. A look of surprise and then disappointment comes over his face and he directs his attention at me. I recline in my seat, completely aware that the boy is now making faces and obscene gestures toward me.

Either the store is crowded or Tammy can't decide between tuna or turkey. I envision her standing there with tuna in one hand and turkey in the other, reading the nutrition facts and trying to figure out which one I'll prefer. I don't care. I just want to be back on the road and I want this bothersome kid to disappear.

The boy's faces fail to get a rise out of me and he starts chanting: "Blackie man, blackie man. Wake up, blackie man." I open my eyes to see his face pressed against the window that's lowered a crack. His nostrils are flared upward and wide like a pig. He's hysterical, laughing and singing the song that won't end—over and over: "Blackie man, blackie man. Wake up, blackie man." I remember the crowbar that's wrapped in a towel in the trunk. I wrapped it in a towel because it was making such a racket when Tammy took corners. I get out and look around the parking lot to make sure no one is watching. The boy gauges my size, his eyes ascending from my feet to my face. He stops singing. I must look like a giant to him.

The illusion of safety is gone and the only thing between us is glass—just glass. The reality of this is evident in the boy's expression. He moves away from the window and returns to the passenger seat. I take a few steps toward the trunk of the Caddy. I look back at the boy and the cabin looks empty. I assume he's on the truck floor, balled up in his arms, eyes shut tight. The way kids toss bedsheets over their heads to protect them from the bad men of their nightmares.

"Well, isn't that sweet of you? You got out to help."

Tammy has a way of sneaking up on me. I turn around to see her arms full of groceries.

"I thought you were getting sandwiches?" I say.

"They had some detergent and things on sale. You know, things are cheaper down here."

I take the bags from her and she lifts the trunk. I load the bags in and get back into the car. Tammy begins to reverse, and I wait for the boy to pop his head up and make one last ugly face, but he doesn't.

"Should we fill up now?" Tammy asks.

"No, we're fine. We can fill up in Virginia."

"Okay," she says. She starts the car and slowly backs out of the space.

"How much were the groceries?" I ask.

Tammy doesn't respond—too busy wrestling with the steering wheel, trying to straighten the Caddy.

"It's time for an alignment, I think," she says.

"Did you hear me?"

"Yes, Paul. I heard you." She shifts into drive. "Since when do you care about how much groceries cost?"

"Since now," I say. "So how much was it? You said things are cheaper down here."

"I think forty-five, maybe fifty dollars."

"Okay," I say.

"Okay? That's all, just okay?"

"I was curious."

"Do you want to talk, Paul? I mean, we don't have to drive the next eight hours in complete silence."

"Talk about what?"

"Your grandfather. You did just bury him. And you didn't even—"

"What, Tammy?"

"You didn't even shed a tear, Paul. I know he meant a lot to you."

"Tears stopped flowing a long time ago."

Tammy sighs. I've exhausted her. She adjusts the air-conditioning setting so it blows colder and then gases the Caddy with a stomp of the foot peddle.

I didn't used to care about money, but it has been on my mind lately—a lot has. I never imagined myself being taken care of, not the way that Tammy cares for me. Some men—the type that sit on the sofa all day drinking, smoking, watching cable TV, and circling a few employment ads in the newspapers just to keep their old ladies off their backs—would love to be in my shoes. But Tammy never causes waves about me not working. It's like some unspoken arrangement—she doesn't bring it up, not even to her girlfriends. She sees me as damaged goods, too damaged to interact with the public, like some dog rescued from a fighting ring—maladjusted and still nursing my wounds. Besides, in this economy, a felon seeking gainful and legal employment is beyond laughable.

Tammy has been my bread and butter since I quit working at the clinic. My boss always had a weakness for her—constantly winking and smiling. Once he learned of our relationship, he figured he would stick it to me the best way he could. Tammy and I had shared the same lunch break since my first day on the job. While I washed bedsheets soiled with piss and sweat, my boss sat behind a desk reading health magazines and drinking herbal tea. He couldn't stand that I was with her—Paul, the ex-con, the lush. So he changed my lunch schedule so it didn't coincide with hers. Then I caught him touching her in a way I didn't like. He was showing her some type of chart when he ran his fingers down the side of her arm. It was subtle, and I could tell Tammy was willing to let it pass, but I wasn't.

I don't remember much, except the sound of the tendons in his arm giving way and then snapping like a handful of Popsicle sticks. His eyes bucked, his skin flushed, his mouth salivated. Later, Tammy told me that he developed a twitch in his right eye and that his pupils stayed glued to the floor whenever she passed. He was like the victim of a school bully, hugging the hallway walls, avoiding eye contact, and flinching when startled or approached from behind. I never understood why he didn't press charges, but he did take a restraining order out against me. I didn't wait for the clinic to investigate. I resigned and spared Tammy more embarrassment. She felt guilty about the hurt I put on him. So she tried to make it all right by prompting idle chitchat about the weather and late-night talk shows in the employees lounge. But nothing seemed to spark the old affinity he once had for her—the twinkle in his eye. I know now that Tammy resented me for taking that away, because it's what I couldn't give her. I've never been much of a romantic; for me a relationship has to be handled pragmatically—it just needs to function.

The hum of the engine and the heat are putting me to sleep. I rest my head back and close my eyes, but it does no good. With every bump and wheel jerk, my head knocks forward and to the side—sometimes knocking against the window so hard that Tammy pesters me making sure I'm all right. Why can't she keep it smooth? She's so goddamn jumpy. It takes about an hour before Tammy finally settles the Caddy into a steady driving rhythm. I'm reluctant to nap, believing at any moment the jerkiness will return.

A brief nap during the drive is the closest I've gotten to sleep in the past few months. At night, I stare up at Tammy's bedroom ceiling while she sleeps soundly next to me. I strained my eyes so bad that one night I thought I saw a face. No particular face, but I could make out the eyes, ears, nose, and a crooked smile. Tammy doesn't know I see things in the shadows. She claims I keep things from her and if I do it's for her own good. The first night we made love she told me that I had a gentle spirit and that I'd make a good father. I wonder how much of that she still believes.

Tammy pumps the brakes hard, and I jolt. The traffic seems to have come out of nowhere and I can see billows of smoke up ahead.

"Must be some kind of wreck," Tammy says.

I pull down the sun visor, shielding the glare so I can get a better look, as we creep closer to the mess ahead of us. A state trooper is laying flares and directing cars to the left of the wreck. A tractor-trailer is on its side. Under it is the front of a crumpled station wagon. The cabin of the wagon is partially intact, but the windows have all been blown out.

"Looky Lou's, people breaking their necks to see this," she says with disgust.

Tammy keeps her eyes on the road, not even stealing a

glance at the carnage ahead and to the right of her. The sedan in front of us is creeping along slowly. The state trooper is blowing his whistle incessantly and waving his arm forward in frustration, but the driver keeps straining for a look.

"My God, what's so exciting about this?" Tammy asks.

"He could be making sure he doesn't know the car," I say.

"Please, they're nosy like everybody else."

"Maybe people slow down to pray."

"That's a nice thought," she says.

Tammy flashes me a smile. She likes it when I talk about God and prayer. I don't believe most of what I hear in church. I've always thought being a preacher was just another con I never had the courage to attempt, but Tammy accredits church for keeping us together.

We're closer now, and I can see smoke coming from the bottom of the station wagon. There are specs of red all over the tan interior. I can smell the blood in the air—the taint like rusted metal. It's splattered on the windshield, the pavement, the white wall of the tire and rim. Strands of hair and pieces of fabric are snagged on shards of glass. There are personal articles littered on the highway: reading glasses, a paperback book, an aluminum coffee mug, a yellow beret, and a small muscled action figure.

"Baby, don't look," she says.

There are three bodies covered with white sheets. Blood has seeped through and looks like the first strokes in an abstract painting. A man's leather loafer sticks out from under the sheet. His foot is twisted and the loafer is saturated with blood. It's a deep burgundy, like it's been soaked in a cheap red wine. Around the body are small pools of blood. The saturated shoe is creating a stream that trickles into a tiny pool, probably formed by a severed artery or severe laceration.

"Paul, did you hear me?"

I can't seem to turn away—the bodies are fresh, two small children and a man, perhaps their father.

"Paul, please don't look."

Tammy tries to cover my eyes with the palm of her hand, but I bat it away. I take her by the wrist tightly, my fingernails dig deep into her skin and I force her hand back on the wheel.

"Keep your hands on the wheel before we end up like them," I say.

There is sharpness in my voice and Tammy's face can't hide her hurt. She bites her lower lip and runs her fingers over her wrist, feeling the indention my fingernails left behind. Her wrist swells a little and I know it'll leave a mark. If it weren't for this wreck, none of this would have happened. Why couldn't we have kept driving? No stops, no traffic, and no bodies. I wish I could take back moments in time—an exchange that would allow me to retrieve minutes from my past for the minutes of my future. So the word mistake would never exist. I never wanted to hurt Tammy, but I've been fighting this day and welcoming it at the same time. Now she can see what I really am. Tammy suffers from blind faith, but I know our relationship has slipped into a coma. We are dying and when that final hour falls there will be no resuscitation.

We sit idle for about thirty minutes. There's only the sound of Tammy grinding her teeth and clearing the back of her throat, something she does when she's angry. I wait for the opportune moment to speak, when her face calms and her frown loosens. Tammy told me once that I was robbing her of her sweetness. I asked her why she bothered with me. She just shut the bedroom door and locked it. That night I slept in my La-Z-Boy.

"I'm sorry," I say.

Tammy ignores me. She looks forward, keeping her hands tight on the wheel. The paramedics are loading the bodies into the coroner's van, and the trooper has successfully diverted traffic to the farthest lane. Tammy needs a guy like the trooper, a man who is good at his role—a server, a protector. A man she can count on.

"I didn't mean it to come out that way," I say. "It just did."

She stays silent and taps her thumb against the wheel.

"Well, just know I'm sorry," I say.

"What?"

"I'm sorry, I said."

"You know what, Paul . . ."

I wait for her to put her Christianity on the shelf and curse me with a few choice words. But she doesn't. Instead, she looks at me fixed. In her eyes: anger and sadness. It makes me so uncomfortable that I'm forced to look away. I've never hurt Tammy. I've never laid a hand on her until now, but in the past few months it's become increasingly easy to enter a forbidden territory. I'm no abuser. I don't take shots at women. I don't use them as punching bags. But I've got an ailment. Some kind of rage deep in the murkiness of my gut and I'm afraid if I don't part from Tammy, she may get the brunt of it. Every time I get angry, pieces of me seem to peel away like layers of paint on a weathered fence and when the paint is gone, when the bare is shown, what will I be?

CHAPTER TWO

We merge onto Broad Street off Interstate 95. Philly is hell in the summer and it reeks of cooked garbage. The stench settles in your clothes like sulfur. Tammy likes the air-conditioning, but I keep the windows down. I've gotten used to the smell. I've spent most of my life in the city, cramped in all corners. At night the summer air is pleasant, it's alive, bustling and sensual. People walk the streets and drink nightcaps on their stoops. The street peddlers harmonize and play catchy tunes on busy corners. When the sun sets, Tammy and I take cold showers and lie naked. We keep the fan propped in front of the window so that it circulates in fresh air. Sometimes we play jazz records and Solomon Burke into the early morning hours. Or we relax on the roof, drinking iced tea, overlooking the skyline.

Tammy makes a left onto Walnut Street. Our apartment is just off 17th Street. It's rough maneuvering the Cadillac in heavy traffic, but Tammy has gotten better at it. People cut in and out, between bumper and fender. Philly's nosier than the South: sirens, horns, whistle blows, shouts, and the wail of a wet trumpet or a winded sax—it's home.

It takes Tammy twenty minutes to find a parking space on the street large enough to accommodate the Caddy. I remove the luggage and my grandfather's things from the trunk and we walk a block to our third-floor apartment. By the time we reach our door, I'm panting and desperate for a cigarette.

Once inside, I set the luggage down, get a bottle of water from the fridge and light up a smoke.

Our apartment is minimal: an easy chair, a loveseat, a coffee table, and an antique floor lamp. Tammy got rid of our television after it broke and cost too much to repair. She found a classic record player and crates of jazz records outside an apartment building that was being torn down. The city was demolishing it because a week before a girl had fallen through the fourth floor. Sometimes I think Philly is too old for living—old buildings, old streets, and an old hopelessness.

Tammy goes into the bedroom to unpack her luggage. She re-emerges with her hair pinned neatly in a bun. She looks like Egyptian royalty with her hair up, or at least what I imagine an Egyptian queen to look like. She uses two chopsticks as pins and leaves a few strands of hair loose and untamed.

Tammy has a sensibility all her own. Sometimes we joke that she's been here before, like an old soul. She always says that she wants to get it right this time—life that is. I once found a postcard dated 1955 at a hand-me-down store. It was a photo of a woman buying fruit in the Italian Market on 9th Street. The woman had an uncanny resemblance to Tammy. I brought the postcard home to show her and ever since then she's convinced it was her soul buying fruit that day fifty some years earlier.

She gets her superstition honestly. Her father was a Puerto Rican cabbie who believed in Santeria, and her mother was a mulatto nurse from New Orleans who blamed her brother's bowel cancer on an old flame's voodoo hex. They fell in love during a cab ride through South Philly. Every morning he'd pick her up so she didn't have to hail a cab. He brought her coffee and breakfast that he had made and packed it so it was nice and hot by the time he got her to work. Eight months later they were married. Tammy was birthed from love and beauty. Who couldn't love her? It's me who is a spawn of something unfit, something unnatural, a mistake between a man, a woman, and God. Some nights I hear Tammy praying before bed. I've never had the audacity to ask her what she prays for, when she prays for me, but I figure she's trying to barter with God on my behalf.

I loved Tammy. I wanted to give her my heart, my soul—lay it flat so she could study it, dissect it, see me for what I was, and fall in love with what she saw. I convinced myself that if I could have her and lie with her, that she would be my fix, my elixir—my cure. But I've failed, I haven't brought her happiness. On most days her love resembles pity. I've been a barnacle on the hull, maybe even a parasite, devouring all in my path and for that I hope she will forgive me, because I've robbed her of her chance to meet a man who could truly love her. But she isn't without hope. Tammy is a beacon of light, capable of enticing men by the droves. In time she could forget me and having found the right man, she could think of me as a bad dream—painful and haunting at the time, but now inconsequential.

● ● ●

We have smothered pork chops, rice, and salad for dinner, along with a bottle of red wine I had picked up from the corner store a few days earlier. Tammy has a glass and leaves the bottle for me to finish. There's no cold shower or jazz tonight; I can tell Tammy is still upset over our argument in the car. She clears the table and washes up the dishes.

"Are you all right?" I ask.

"I'm just tired," she says. "That drive took a lot out of me."

Tammy goes into the bathroom and runs herself a bath. I flip through a book about purchasing land on unclaimed islands. I picked it up at a newsstand on Walnut two days ago, after reading an article about stockbrokers who've been buying private islands and selling them off by the acre. I figured I wouldn't need much room—my prison cell was 8 by 10 feet. Tammy opens the bathroom door. The scent of vanilla bath oil travels into the living room, followed by Tammy wrapped in a terry cloth robe and slippers.

"I'm going to lie down after my bath," she says.

"I'll probably join you in a while," I say.

Tammy doesn't refute, and I'm grateful for not having to sleep in the La-Z-Boy, given the hurt the long car ride put on my back.

I put the book down and head into the kitchen to make some tea. I let the tea cool and drop a few ice cubes into my glass. I perch myself on the windowsill and watch people, cars, and taxi cabs pulsate through the city streets the way blood pumps through veins. It's two-dollar beer night at the local dive. Which means it's alive with off-duty cops, college kids, and drunken businessmen—a potent mix for trouble when the witching hour comes. Just outside the door, intoxicated patrons drop bills into a saxophonist's hat. Some are too drunk to realize they're giving up their cab fare. Everybody loves everybody when liquor is involved and the bums know it. They hover around the bar waiting for the loudest, drunkest, most slaphappy fool to come out singing and dancing in the street. Just eager to make everyone feel as good as he does and what better way than to give up a few dollar bills.

The streets have changed since I used to run them. The alleys are cleaner and the smut has moved south onto 13th Street. For a five spot you used to be able to get your jimmy yanked by a lady and have enough for a shot or two after. Now you better be prepared to spend and make sure it's a woman who is doing the yanking. Once I tried to tell Tammy about my life on the street before I got locked up. I didn't get halfway into my story before she changed the subject and served me a piece of hot apple pie with ice cream. I just figured it was too much for her. Sometimes it isn't good to show someone your world if they aren't ready to peek.

I lie down next to Tammy. I can't tell if she's asleep or just resting. The moon highlights the contours of her body. Her nightgown clings tightly to her skin and accents every curve and subtle detail, I long to touch her. I run my fingers down the side of her arm and rest my hand below her waist. Before touching Tammy I often envision how the sex will go. I think about the parts of her body I can touch that will elicit certain responses. I learned touching her on her hip means we'll make love. It'll be soft, gentle, and slow. She'll climax after thirty minutes and then she'll fall right asleep.

Kissing her on her neck means it'll be passionate and long. Sometimes we'll move to different locations in the apartment, like the kitchen, the loveseat, or the small corner between the door and the coat closet.

Caressing her breasts and squeezing them tightly, grabbing the back of her neck when kissing her and running my hand between her thighs leads to screwing. It's never soft and gentle. It's painful and cathartic. It leaves our bodies battered and bruised. For Tammy and me this is rare. The conditions have to be just right, meaning she has to have had a bad day at the clinic or some pervert has come onto her in the drugstore. Whatever it is, it has to bring about some pain. Then she comes home and we screw, until the details of the day blur like an obsolete memory.

She turns to face me and pulls me close, she kisses me and we have sex—an empty, meaningless sex with a dearth of emotion. Hours later, she's cradled in my arms. Our bodies contorted like origami folds, my leg under hers, hers over mine. I'm staring up at the ceiling trying to make sense out of the shadows. I can hear the boys outside, liquored up and playing loaded dice games for bragging rights and a fist full of dollars. The constant clacking of ivory dice hitting the concrete is bouncing off the bedroom walls.

Clack, clack and clack.

I want to go out there and tell them to quiet down, but moving will only disturb her. Maybe Tammy is right? Maybe I am losing my mind? Maybe a sin is coming on something terrible and I don't want her around when it happens? What if the streets are calling and my life out there isn't finished? What if there's an ill part of me still living, still breathing, like a caged beast that's been poked, prodded, and starved—and it wants out? What if I was never meant to inhabit the body of a man? What if my calling is a wild one? Unchained, like a stray dog running the alleys and fighting in the backstreets, a beast.

It's a typical lazy Sunday. Tammy is out for her morning run. I grab the newspaper from the stoop and head into the kitchen to make myself breakfast. I fry some turkey bacon and eggs and toast a slice of whole wheat bread that Tammy purchased at a gourmet market. I have a glass of orange juice with heavy pulp and a cup of coffee, black. I take a seat in my usual place on the windowsill. The humidity has already set in, and I can tell by the afternoon it's going to feel like an oven. I see Tammy jogging from across the street holding a bag and what looks to be a broomstick in her hands. I unlock the door so I don't have to hear her fumble for her keys, curse and go into a tizzy-fit about how I never open the door for her.

Five minutes later, Tammy comes in carrying a brown bag and a wooden-handled mop. She props the mop against the kitchen counter and starts taking things out of the bag.

"I thought we had a mop?" I ask.

"We do," she says. "This one is special."

I investigate her *special* mop. It looks old and there's wording and glyphs carved into the wood. It's made by hand, with thick woven yarn at the head. Tammy takes out a plastic jug of green liquid from the bag.

"What's that?"

"Lucky floor wash."

"Where's the label?"

"There is no label. They make it in-house."

"Who makes it?"

"The lady down on South Street," she says coyly.

"What's the point?"

"It's going to help with the vibe of the apartment."

"The vibe?"

Tammy puts the floor wash under the kitchen sink and starts straightening up, shuffling magazines and shifting things around.

"Well, I went into a shop. You know that shop with all the occult books and love potions? And the lady said it helps with mood and I figured it wouldn't hurt to try."

I stay silent and return to my windowsill. Tammy goes

into the bedroom and changes her clothes. She comes out moments later in denim cut-off shorts and her hair pulled back in a ponytail. She heads for the kitchen carrying a bucket from under the bathroom sink.

"You're mopping now?" I ask.

"Sure, why not?"

She pops the seal on the floor wash and it releases a pungent aroma. It smells of rotten fruit. Tammy can sense that I'm restless, but this magic floor wash is desperation. She dips the mop into the bucket and begins to scrub an already clean floor. I get up and retreat to the bedroom.

I pick up a photo of Tammy and me that's sitting on the nightstand, and take a seat on the bed. It's a photo of our vacation in Puerto Rico. It's the last time I remember being happy, before this torment began. I walk to the closet and take out the green duffle bag I purchased from the army surplus store six months ago. I start packing it with clothes, clean underwear, and my shaving kit. I can hear Tammy in the kitchen still vigorously scrubbing the floor. I keep packing, putting in a few dress shirts and slacks. I take out my polish and brush and shine up my dress loafers. I pace the room—back and forth, back and forth. I don't know how much time passes or why I don't hear Tammy come in. I turn and face her. She's standing in the doorway with that all too familiar look on her face—anger, surprise, disappointment.

"What are you doing?" she asks.

Tammy knows the answer before she even asks the question. Her face tells the truth. She knows I'm leaving and there's nothing that can change that, especially not a bottle of floor wash. She approaches and takes a seat on the bed.

"Can I have a cigarette?" she asks.

I take a cigarette from the pack and hand it to her. I light it with my last match and she inhales slowly. Tammy never smokes. It's strange watching her puff away nonchalantly, the white smoke seeping out of the tight slanted opening of her lips.

"So, where are you going?" she asks.

I don't have an answer for her. I watch the cigarette burn slow and hang loose and defiant from her lower lip. She's sweating and her clothes are stained with the green floor wash. She walks over to the window and turns on the fan that's on the sill. She pauses to look in the duffle bag—running her hands through its contents.

"I bought you this shaving kit and now you're leaving!"

I want to speak, but my tongue sits heavy in my mouth, like it's swollen up twice its normal size. The lump in my throat is an apple core, and beads of sweat are starting to form on my knuckles.

"I've just got to go away for a while."

The words come out before I give them much thought. I'm like a puppet on a string. I look around for the ventriloquist, but it's only Tammy, the duffle bag, and me.

"Two days till you're off probation; I suppose you were just waiting for this?"

"I've been feeling it for some time. . . ."

"What are you going to do? Change your name? Disappear?"

"No, my name stays. It has my grandfather's blood on it."

"You won't last a day on your own," she says.

I pick up the duffle bag and sling it over my shoulder. Tammy smokes the cigarette to the butt and then flicks it out of the window.

"Do you have money?" she asks.

"Some," I say.

"How much?" she asks.

"One hundred dollars and thirty-seven cents," I answer, proudly.

She chuckles scornfully.

I take a step forward and she takes two steps toward me. We're toe-to-toe and I can smell her smoke-laced breath. She's breathing hard. It feels like at any moment she is going to pounce on me. I anticipate it, but her act of aggression comes in the form of a smile. Then she moves aside.

"I guess that's something you didn't get from your grandfather. He wasn't a coward. He wouldn't have done this. And you call yourself a man. I'll never forgive you."

I try to ignore her and keep walking, but she knocks the duffle bag out of my hands and it crashes to the floor. I pick it up and this time my grip is firm. Tammy grabs for the duffle bag again, but my hands are too tight on the strap. Her elbow slams into my chin. I grab Tammy by the arm and push her to the floor. She falls back into the nightstand. There's more satisfaction on her face than horror. My actions have solidified the end of us. Maybe now she can break from me clean, maybe now she can hate me.

I keep moving toward the door. She stays seated on the floor, her knees pulled into her chest, weeping. She follows me with her eyes. I face her one last time. I long for her to curse me again. She doesn't and I leave.

I stand outside a few minutes, looking up at my perching window before hailing a cab: a dingy yellow heap with a Jamaican flag hanging from the rearview mirror. I get in and slide my duffle bag to the corner of the seat.

"Where to?" the cabbie asks.

"Dooney's Barber Shop. North Philly."

The cab heads north on Broad Street. He has the air-conditioning blowing full blast.

"Is it all right if I roll down the window?" I ask.

"You sure, buddy? It's blazing hot out there."

"I'm sure."

I roll down the window and take in the smells of the city: the hot dog vendors and grease trucks, the exhaust fumes, and the occasional cigarette trails. I inhale it all so that it becomes a part of me, so it's in my blood—my system.

"Right or left, buddy?" asks the cabbie.

"Right."

The cab bears right and parks in front of Dooney's. He puts on his flashers. I pay him a ten spot and two bucks for tip. I grab my duffle bag and get out. I walk toward the shop. There's a circle of boys hanging out in front. I find a gap in the circle and squeeze in. One of the boys notices me right away. My presence alone seems to entertain him. A pompous grin forms across his face. He crosses his arms and sizes me up.

"What do you know about the boom-bap?" he asks.

"What?"

"Hip-hop. You stepped in the cipher, didn't you?"

"The cipher?" I ask.

"Yeah, the circle, the rotation," he says, somewhat perturbed.

"Man, I just needed a light."

The boys are passing around what I thought was a cigarette from the distance of the cab, but now I can see it's a joint. Each boy takes two puffs and then passes it along.

"So, soldier, you going to spit something?" he asks.

"I don't know."

"Spit about war."

My military duffle bag and work boots has the boy convinced I'm a soldier.

"Fine, we'll come around to you," he says.

The boy takes a swig from his water bottle and then wipes his mouth with his shirt. He closes his eyes and raises his hand to his chest.

"I was birthed in a Philadelphia crime time/where liquor and weed brought peace to my mind/I used to pass time from a downtown roof top/Careful when I blazed/Had to watch for cops/Below/ Footsteps from block-to-block/My symphony of chaos/Smiles and cries/Sirens and cherries 'sposed to mean the good guys/But that ain't the case/ Murder is the case/They never gave me/They hate me/And on a late night/ I had a vision/The bills were due/So I stole the life of a young blue suit. . . ."

The cipher erupts into a monolithic "Ooohhh." The boy smiles and then takes another sip from his water bottle.

"Your turn."

The boy looks at me, waiting to either be impressed or for me to buckle under pressure.

"Okay," I say.

I pause for a moment and then recite a haiku I memorized years ago. The boys are silent and search each other's faces for reactions—then they break into hysterical laughter.

"Ah man, it didn't even rhyme and it wasn't long enough," he says, before tossing me a lighter. I light my cigarette and toss it back to him.

"Thanks for the light."

"Hey, you earned it," he says. "That's the best laugh I've had all week." I head into the shop.

Dooney's shop is always busy. There's a line of patrons waiting along the wall. They're sitting, standing, and some hovering around a small rabbit-ears television with a fuzzy picture and a bent coat hanger for an antenna. A tall fella, probably in his mid-twenties is talking and has Dooney's full attention. He's sloppy, wearing a basketball jersey that reads the name *Wallace* on the back and a pair of oversized denim shorts that hang low, exposing his dingy stripped boxer shorts. When he speaks, he stands upright as if delivering an important speech to an awaiting public, and when something excites him, he waves his hands in awkward motions and pumps his fist. He's got the mouth of a man who has never spent longer than a night in county—he doesn't even stop to catch his breath. On the inside, the first rule of survival is knowing when to shut up—a lesson this kid hasn't learned.

"So, what did you tell her?" Dooney asks.

"To leave," he says.

Dooney takes a break from cutting a customer's hair and rolls his wrist around in a half-circle motion, cringing slightly from the discomfort. He oils his clippers and then goes back to cutting.

"And you really threw her clothes out the window?" Dooney asks.

"Hell, yeah! She's probably out drinking and God knows what else with my kid in her belly. I sent her to her mother's house. But truth be told, I'm not even sure it's my kid."

"That's cold, Marcus. Who else's kid would it be?"

"Shit, man. Who knows? But if it is my kid, I'm gonna do right by him. I'm gonna get my cash up and he'll never want for anything."

"It's good to hear you talking sense, taking some responsibility," Dooney says.

"I want better, Dooney. I'm tired of living like this, scraping for pennies, hustling in these streets."

"You just have to find what you're good at—find an honest, legal gig. You can always work for me. I could use a steady hand."

"That's nice, Dooney, but you've seen me cut. This place would close in a day."

Dooney chuckles, "Ah, you just need barber schooling. Nothing I couldn't teach you here, though."

Dooney's shop has always been a safe haven for ex-cons. Dooney has a soft spot for them, considering he did a ten-year stint back in the '80s for manslaughter. It's also a good place to find work, street jobs for a quick hundred spot. But it's a place where you don't want to get too loose, too comfortable. It is common knowledge that when you walk into Dooney's, there are a few under-covers hanging about, hidden among the patrons. Sometimes you can point them out. The rookies never make direct eye contact and usually flip through magazines or make small talk with the guy next to them. They work at it, like they've never been in a barbershop before, or around ex-cons. But the more seasoned cops are harder to spot. It's best to look at how they stand. A veteran cop with a military background can't shake certain idiosyncrasies. He's so used to standing at attention and commanding authority that he'll slip into a heel-to-toe stance without noticing. It may be only for a moment, but it's all you need to discern friend from foe and to operate safely in Dooney's.

Some of the men have even developed code words, interlaced with slang that can be used to set up drops or meeting places. At Dooney's you feel safe, like you're among like-minded men. Unified by an experience the way cancer survivors have support groups. But prison is never discussed. It's not even hinted at. On the surface, it just looks like a bunch of fellas waiting for haircuts and shooting the proverbial shit. It's all about the words behind the words—what isn't said.

Dooney finishes up with his customer, brushing the few balls of hair from his neck with a talc brush. He notices me out of the corner of his eye and quickly sets the brush down on the counter behind him.

"Youngblood!"

I walk toward him and rest my duffle bag at my feet. I give him a hug.

"It's been a while," I say.

Dooney's arms are beefy and chiseled. All those years of cutting blood-fades and crafting sharp caesars have left him with arthritis and carpal tunnel. His thumbs curve, as if gravity or some unseen force is pulling them back, and his knuckles are knotted and purple. He's a round-bellied gentle giant, whose love handles spill over his waistband like bread with too much yeast.

Dooney takes a twenty from his customer and thanks him for his business. Seconds later, Marcus hops up, brushes past me, and climbs into the barber chair.

"Did you jump ahead?" asks Dooney.

"Come on, Dooney, I've been waiting for an hour."

Marcus looks at me with faint familiarity.

"I know you?" he asks.

"No, we've never met," I say.

He studies me for a moment, his eye cocked upward and glaring.

"Well, you have now," Dooney says. "Paul, this is Marcus Wallace. The fool with two first names."

I shake Marcus' hand and follow his gaze over to the corner of the shop. A man dressed in a black business suit and a crisp white shirt, with silver reading frames poking out of his left breast pocket, is staring in our direction. He's balding and there's a heavy shine on his forehead where his hair has receded. His mustache is thin and probably took him an hour to shape. Each side is measured with precision and there's sheen to the hair, like it's been slicked down with pomade.

Marcus winks at me. He's giving me the heads up that the businessman is watching our interaction. The man seems too clean, too manicured to be a cop—unless he's a fed? I position myself so he gets a hard view of my back.

"So, what's your hobby?" Marcus asks.

"Nothing special," I say. "I like to watch things."

"Watch things?" he asks. "Like television?"

"More like bird watching, without the birds."

"How long have you been out of work?" he asks.

"Too long," I say.

"The economy is real bad. You ever deliver Chinese?"

"Once or twice, but I've got no wheels," I say.

I pull back some. Marcus is overly inquisitive.

"You ever dig a ditch?" he asks.

Dooney sneers at him, but he continues.

"A long time ago," I say.

"That right?"

Dooney nudges Marcus and he finally gets the hint.

I take a seat in the empty barber chair to the right of them. Marcus relaxes, and Dooney wraps the thin white paper around his neckline.

It's true, Marcus is a fool with two first names: he stumbled through the street lingo and his questions were loaded and came too soon apart, an amateur posing as a thoroughbred.

"How do you like my wall of fame?" Dooney asks. "It's grown since the last time you were here."

The barbershop walls are decorated with signed photos of Philly's famous: Solomon Burke, Will Smith, DJ Jazzy Jeff, Bill Cosby, and the Mayor to name a few.

"I think Solomon was your first photo."

"That's right. You're sharp. It's really growing isn't it?"

"Yeah, it's really growing," I say.

I walk over to the water cooler and pass the businessman, who is now reading a trend magazine with an attractive girl on the cover. I fill my Dixie cup twice before returning to my seat. A short older man with salt-and-pepper hair comes in holding a cardboard box filled with hot lunches.

"What's up, Left?" Dooney asks.

Left cracks a toothless smile and drags his right leg across the scuffed linoleum.

"I've got lunch plates," he says, "fish, chicken, and ribs. Five dollars."

A few fellas waiting for cuts dig into their pockets and take out five-dollar bills and change.

"Don't go spending your haircut money now," Dooney says half jokingly.

The fellas chuckle and then hand Left their money.

"You hungry?" Dooney asks.

"No, I'm fine."

"You sure?"

I nod and Dooney goes back to cutting. I keep my eyes on the businessman, who keeps his face buried in the magazine.

Left counts up his money and then heads out, whistling a tune and dragging his bad leg down the block.

The men rip into the plastic cutlery and the sound of persistent chatter is now replaced with a persistent chomping, and the occasional "That's good," like a congregation saying amen when the preacher hits a truth. I watch them eat and I get glimpses of who they were behind bars. The way they guard their food with their arms, like they're still fighting to protect their scraps in the mess hall. Or the way they glance up periodically and keep their plastic knives low and tight in their fists.

It's impossible to purge prison completely, but for a few hours these men can forget.

The businessman's phone rings and the men ice up. Everyone looks at him as if his phone ring is the go signal for some sting operation. He silences the ring, gets up, and rushes out of the shop. The men resume eating. I look back at Dooney, who shrugs and continues with Marcus' cut. I rest my head back and close my eyes. I doze off to the chomping and the buzz of Dooney's clippers.

For hours, time carries on without me. I stir. My eyelids flutter open. Slivers of fluorescent light cut in between lash and lid. The shop comes into focus, and I can make out Dooney's broom swinging back and forth, gathering up balls of hair into the dustpan. I wipe the sleep from my eyes with my shirtsleeve and stretch my legs, rotating my ankles until they crack and pop.

"You must have been tired."

"What time is it?" I ask.

"About eight," Dooney says, glancing at his watch.

The shop is empty. Dooney's has been closed for three hours. I look outside. The sun is setting and throwing bold oranges, purples, and reds across the dim sky.

"You really knocked out," Dooney says.

"Sorry," I say.

"Have you been sleeping?"

"Not really."

"You don't have that narco . . . naraco—"

"Narcolepsy, no, I don't have that."

I get up and walk over to the water cooler. I pour myself a cup of water, take it down and then toss the Dixie cup into the trash. Dooney puts his broom down and then takes my duffle bag out from the cabinet behind the barber chairs.

"I didn't want someone snatching it."

He hands it to me and I thank him.

"You still plugged with that Spanish dame?" he asks.

Sometimes it's easier to feed a lie when part of you still believes it. I guess I wanted to imagine that Tammy was home waiting up for me and keeping me safe with her prayers. The way a wife prays for her soldier husband off at war. But on the contrary, Tammy is busy erasing me from her life—everything that holds my scent, all the remnants of my presence, and the reminders of our failed life together. Like lifting a stain from her favorite blouse, she'll work at it until it's like I was never there.

I tell Dooney things are fine between us and he accepts the short answer.

"I should go," I say.

Dooney sweeps up the last bit of hair into the dustpan and then tosses it into the trash. He stretches his fingers out and then retracts them into his palm to make a fist. With a sigh, he says, "Sometimes I think getting old isn't such a blessing."

"You ever think about retiring?" I ask. "Leaving this city for good?"

"Retirement is a luxury I don't have. I've got no pension, no 401K. I'm just a broke barber trying to keep his shop afloat and, most likely, I'll die that way."

He reaches out to shake my hand, but instead pulls me close and then wraps his arm around me.

"But if you need anything don't you hesitate," he says. "You know I'd do anything for you."

"I could go for a light," I say.

Dooney reaches into his pocket and produces a silver butane lighter. He brings it to the tip of my cigarette and lights it. The flame flickers and then runs down the side, almost scarring it to its filter. I take a drag.

"That fella who was in here," he says, "the one wearing the suit. . . ."

"Sure, what about him?"

"He's been in and out, says he has a job, easy cash."

"Really?" I say. "He sure rushed out of here in a hurry."

"He spooks easy," he says.

"You know him well?"

"Sure, he's solid," Dooney says.

"What kind of job is he talking?"

"Not sure. How bad do you need money?"

"As bad as any man, I guess. But I'll make do." I pat Dooney on the back and head out with my cigarette resting in the crescent of my mouth.

Outside I notice a parked car sitting idle a few blocks down from the barbershop. Its lights are cut off, but I can make out the figure of a man wearing a crooked cap on the driver's side. A sign points east directing me to a subway terminal. Maybe I can ride the train for a bit, get my head together, work out a plan. I'm about six blocks from the terminal and a mild breeze has set in. I smoke my cigarette slow, relaxing in the moment. The breeze brushes against my skin and it's the only reprieve I've gotten from the heat all day. I'm not even two blocks in and my dogs are already starting to ache. Tammy picking me up and dropping me off places has spoiled me. She was always afraid I'd become a victim of a stick-up kid or a needle freak. Or perhaps one night I just wouldn't come home. Tammy was always there, sitting at a corner or double-parked, waiting.

I didn't hear the footsteps over the breeze rustling littered newspapers and tossing empty beer cans about in the street. I'm not sure how long I had been followed, but the footsteps are coming steady and fast. There's urgency in them, and I move to the right of the sidewalk, hoping the person will pass. Instead, the steps adjust with mine, shifting to the right and then dropping back a few paces. If this is a robbery, he could be getting his confidence up before he leaps. Or he could be biding his time, searching for a section of street he's familiar with, something dimly lit and abandoned. I think about turning around and telling him my bag is filled with outdated clothes and prison-issued boxer shorts. But instead I keep moving, doubling my stride. I come up on a cut street and dip in, posting myself flush with the wall of a building. Shrouded in shadow, I quiet my breathing to a faint murmur. I wait till he gets close. Step. Pause. Step. Pause. Step. Pause . . . I count about ten steps before I reach out and snatch him by his shirt collar. I shove him and he crashes into a dumpster. It's too dark to tell if he's out cold. I wait a moment before dragging him into the amber streetlight.

It only takes me seconds to recognize the silver-rimmed glasses in his breast pocket. It's the businessman from Dooney's. I snatch his billfold from his pants. I flip through his credit cards: platinum, gold, silvers. I remove his driver's license. It's a younger photo, thicker hair and less wrinkles. His name: Harlin Washington. I pocket his business card, a white stock with the particulars printed in black raised ink.

"Why are you following me?" I ask.

He's coherent, but jumpy. He lets out a strained gasp and then slides a few inches away from me.

"Easy, just be easy," I say. "What do you want?"

He takes a long deep breath.

"I've got something for you," he says.

I back away from him and look around the alley for anything suspicious. He gets to his feet slowly, moving away from the dumpster that's heaving with rats.

"It's not like that," he says. "It's a job. You're looking for work aren't you?"

The businessman looks me up and down, focusing on my tattered pants and worn boots.

"Maybe," I say.

"Well, it's damn near free money," he says.

"Don't con me."

I start moving away from the alley.

"Wait," he says.

He flashes me a handful of big bills and I stop in my tracks.

"I'm sorry. I'm no good at this. A friend told me if I came down here I could find . . ."

"Save it," I say.

I'm positive he's not a cop, but something about him makes me uneasy. He reeks of expensive cologne and his cuff links are diamond-crafted, and glimmer when they catch the street lamp. He's some kind of rich. I'm just not sure if he's the legal kind.

"I need you to deliver something," he says.

"Do I look like a sucker to you? Go to hell."

"No dope or anything," he says. "I can pay you up front. I'm down to the wire. I've been in and out of that barber shop looking for a guy and it's havoc on my nerves."

"You sound like you're facing heat."

"Just some men I work for. I'm up against a wall. Dooney knows my story. I figured with you two being friends I should take a chance."

"How do you know Dooney?" I ask.

"Just from around, you know how that is? Feel free to check me out with him, he'll tell you."

"How much money are we talking about?" I ask.

"Five hundred up front and one thousand for the total job," he says.

The businessman counts out the money, which is divided into fifties, twenties, and tens.

"Here's five hundred," he says. "I'll pay you another five hundred when it's done."

He takes out a small sheet of paper with an address scribbled in smudged ink. His nerves probably got the better of him and the ink smudged when his palm got sweaty.

"You'll wait at this address. A man will hand it to you, along with where to deliver it. The man will be there at twelve-thirty tomorrow night."

"What's this fella look like?" I ask.

"Don't worry about that. He'll find you."

"And how do I get the other half of the money?" I ask.

"When it's done, you call me. We can arrange to meet at Dooney's. Is that fair?"

"Fair enough," I say.

I put the money in my pocket and walk until my feet hit the sidewalk and the thick smell of cologne is safely in the distance. At the corner I look back and see the green sedan creeping up slowly behind me. The man in the crooked cap rolls down the window and a cloud of white smoke emits from the car.

"You need a ride?"

I recognize the voice.

"No, Marcus. I'm fine."

"You sure? You look lost and it can get hot over here at this hour." I reconsider, taking into account the wad of cash I just shoved into my pocket and the fact my bearings are off. Walking the city isn't like driving it. Things look different and yet the same: red-bricked buildings, concrete and cobblestone, abandoned lots and torn-down street signs. Your mind convinces you the neighborhood is familiar and dawns phony memories, like some lurid déjà vu.

The trunk bounces open, and I put my duffle bag in. I get into the car. Marcus is reclined so far back he can barely see over the steering wheel. There's a dank smell of dope and stale beer. Soda cans litter the floor, along with negative bank statements and fast-food ketchup packets. Marcus ashes his blunt out the window and takes two puffs before offering it to me.

"I don't smoke," I say.

"You sure?" he asks.

"Yes."

Marcus brings the blunt to his mouth with the tips of two fingers and wraps his thick lips around the end. He inhales steady and then lets out a cough that turns into a husky chuckle. The thick fleshy part of his neck jiggles in sync with the chuckle and there's a dark ring of resin around his lips, which has stained his skin.

"How long have you known Dooney?" he asks.

"A while," I say.

Marcus inhales the last bit of the blunt and then flicks the roach out of the window.

"Where you headed?" he asks.

"Nowhere, really, you can drop me off on South and I'll walk."

Marcus eases off the brake and then presses the gas pedal.

"Busy night for you?" he asks.

"Not really," I say.

"I saw you talking to that suited cat from the shop."

"He needed directions."

Marcus cuts his eyes at me and then moistens his chapped lips with his tongue.

"You sure that's all he needed? You know that shop is a sleeper? Fellas come in there for all sorts on the low, all sorts. I say they should take that shit to 13th Street, but that's just my opinion."

Marcus makes the right turn onto Broad Street and heads east. I keep my eyes on the street signs, trying to commit them to memory.

"That businessman is going to put you on, isn't he?" he says. "He's got something cooking, I know it and he's going to put you on."

"He was looking for a good soft pretzel. I sent him up the block."

"You gonna play me like this? Share the wealth. It's dry out here, just queers and dope. Kool-Aid lips and pumps, I tell ya."

"Maybe you should give it a taste if it's that bad," I say, lightly.

"I'm no punk!" Marcus snaps back.

I recognize an Italian joint. The sign features a big-breasted brunette wearing a red tank top holding a pepperoni pie, and the words "hot" and "fresh" rising from the box like steam.

"You can let me out here," I say.

"Here?"

"I'm going to cop a cheesesteak. I haven't had one in a minute."

Marcus slams on his brakes, hits his flashers, and pops the trunk. I get out and crouch low to the cabin.

"Here," he says. "Take this." He hands me a small piece of paper with his phone number scribbled on it.

"In case you change your mind and decide to share the wealth."

"I don't know what you're talking about," I say.

"I smell the lavender on your clothes. Maybe you should go home to whatever hussy you left crying and patch things up?"

"It's nice to know you care," I say.

Marcus sucks his teeth and adds a few syllables to a short curse word. I slam the door and grab my duffle bag out of the trunk. He revs the engine, spitting exhaust and tire smoke, before turning and vanishing down 8th Street. Marcus wanted to leave a sting and he did. It didn't bother me, the hussy comment, but the implication the streets could get the better of me didn't sit well.

I'm no fool. I know the streets have changed, but the rules haven't. Snitches are still snitches and cash is the holiest fabric. But I've failed. I stopped loving her—the streets. We've lost communication. She stopped talking and I stopped listening. How will she forgive my transgression? Nights, I fell to my knees told her my dreams and in turn she infected me: the hustle, the quest, the paper chase—her disease. I was her disciple, maneuvering her maze of alleys, crack houses, queen galleys, chambers of dope, and black markets. Will she take me back, her long-lost lover? Or is my fate already planned? Are my bones set to be added to her temple of demise? Today, mistakes are cemented in blood. I could die in her trap. How many ex-cons have returned to the streets, to her bosom, believing they could be nursed back to health, and how many have had their bones sucked clean?

Shall I do penance, Hail Marys, a baptism?

Speak my name. Give me your blessing, a sign, anything. Tell me I'm still loved. . . .

Nothing, there are no words to be spoken. There is no welcome home. No ceremony. I'm a memory and perhaps it's best we don't get reacquainted.

CHAPTER THREE

A HEAVY MAN WEARING a white greasy apron slides the foil-wrapped chicken steak across the counter.

"It's hot, guy," he says, wiping his sweat-drenched brow with the back of his hand. "That'll be six-fifty."

He notices me staring at the straw he's grinding in his teeth and the tiny pieces of red plastic that are logged between them.

"I'm trying to quit smoking. My nephew said to chew a straw all day."

"Is it working?" I ask.

"I haven't smoked yet. It used to be a pack a day."

I take my time removing the wad of bills from my pocket and picking which president to pay with. I pay with Hamilton, even though I have smaller bills. I figure the singles will come in handy for tipping a cabbie or paying for the bus.

I can't remember the last time I've had money in my

pocket that wasn't Tammy's. I used to hate Tammy shelling out cash for me. Every Friday my billfold would sit heavy in my back pocket. I figured she would stuff it with twenties and tens the night before, like a payroll deposit and come morning the money would be there. Sometimes she would even write tiny words on the border of the bill—the way mothers put notes with feel-good annotations in their kids' lunch boxes. She jotted nice things like: "Have a great day", "See you at dinner", or "You look handsome". It made me sick. I found myself fixing things around the apartment that worked perfectly. I recalibrated the thermostat. I replaced week-old light bulbs. I regrouted the kitchen tile and organized her closet first by color and then alphabetically by designer. Anything to assuage the guilt I felt for not being the breadwinner.

The man hands me my change, leaving a greasy thumbprint on

Lincoln's face. I take a seat in the cleanest booth I can find. I get about ten bites in before noticing the tiny specs of red plastic nestled between meat, cheese, and the extra onions I paid twenty-five cents for. I wrap the sandwich back in its foil. The experience kills my appetite, and scenarios run through my mind of how such a thing could have happened. The first, being an act of malice, like a race thing, or just an asshole thing. The second, an honest mistake, the bits of straw on the chewed end could have easily slid through to the tip making their way into my sandwich. But how could a person not notice a thing like that? After all, he's been chewing that straw all day. My hands are fists on the table, and my fingernails are digging into my palms so deeply that they're starting to break the skin. I want desperately to get up and take the steel napkin holder to his sweaty mug. But I stomach the anger, dump the sandwich into the garbage can and walk out.

I head east to a dive bar called Angel Wings Tavern, a joint as eclectic as its name. The bar is dimly lit with neon beer signs. A manikin dressed in a rainbow-colored wig and lime-green Mardi Gras beads stands in the corner. The bartender is wearing a white collared shirt with a crooked polka-dot bow tie and skinny red suspenders. He looks like the lion wrangler at the circus or the host for a children's program, the kind of show where a goofy fella teaches kids their alphabet or how to add and subtract. He fixes me a strong whiskey and I select a few soul classics in the jukebox: "Midnight Train to Georgia", "Proud Mary", and "Only a Dream". A group of blue-collars make their way toward the bar, their bellies heavy with beer and liquor. A bearded man with dried paint on his coveralls seats himself on a barstool. The bartender pours him a double shot of Jack and he wraps his hand around the shot glass.

"Happy Hour is just about over," he says. "Another drink?"

I nod, and he slides me down a double shot of Jack before putting the bottle away.

"A single is fine," I say.

"It's on the house. You look like you could use it."

I sip the whiskey, savoring the body. I let it linger in the back of my throat and then trickle down to the center of my chest.

"Where you from?" he asks.

"Around."

"What do they call you?"

"Paul."

"I'm Earl."

Earl extends his hand and we shake.

"Nice to meet you."

"Paul, from all around town. . . . I've seen you in here a few times, years back. I thought maybe you stopped drinking, found religion or something."

"I was on vacation," I say.

"I see," he says.

Earl winks. He knows it wasn't a vacation. Bartenders can always smell the stench a prison cell can leave. After all, we're usually their best customers.

"Well, it's good to have you back, Paul."

"Thanks."

Earl goes back to wiping down the bar, and I make my home in some stale pretzels, tossing them into my mouth by the handful. I hear a few snickers behind me and look over my shoulder to see a group of twenty-somethings dressed in thrift store get-ups: tight jeans with faded shirts and '80s race jackets. One of them, a boy wearing a pink polo walks over to the jukebox and drops enough quarters in to last till closing. He tunes it to classic rock and then crosses his eyes at me. I don't pay him any mind.

The whiskey is relaxing me and my thoughts are on my grandfather's farm. It's been on my mind since I left North Carolina, an unyielding vision—I jump reality's ship and find my way back to it. Philly can have my heart, but the South will preserve my soul. Life lies in the land, if I can return to it. If I can make it home, then maybe there is hope.

Philadelphia is an urbanized hub of neighborhoods masquerading as a metropolis. It's an obscene city and it's at war with itself. It feeds on itself like a rat gnawing on the skin and gristle of its tail. Everything in this city is in opposition to what it is to live, and if I'm to have any chance at living, I've got to flee before I become a slave to it. Before I become like everyone else, hollowed out and empty, existing, but far from living.

I've worked out the numbers in my head. A rough estimate of how much it'll take to restore my grandfather's farm and make it like it was: three thousand, four hundred and fifty dollars, give or take, just enough for the much-needed improvements and to re-plant the garden. I figure I can get a friend of my grandfather's, maybe Rally down the road, to help me fix the leaky roof. A few new planks of wood and a saw should run me two hundred dollars. The rotten pipes I can fix myself. It's a simple task of replacing the failing metal pipes with copper ones, which should cost me about one hundred bucks at best. The garden's a cakewalk. A bag of fresh topsoil, some plant food graduals, and rolling up the sleeves. It should run me fifty dollars and a twenty spot to borrow Rally's truck and get down to the garden supply store. The carpet is soiled beyond saving and will need to come up. If I'm lucky, there'll be hardwood underneath and not cement, which would only require a forty-dollar sander and some wood stain. The gravel road desperately needs to be paved and it's the one task that will hurt my pocket the most—five hundred at best. But with the extra bread from the businessman job, I'll have enough to paint the interior walls, refurbish the fireplace, and even fix the wobbly deck that termites have done a number on.

The businessman's job—for a moment I had forgotten about the task only focusing on the pay-off. His proposition is hanging over my head like a nagging schoolteacher. It's a 50/50 chance the play is a setup. The role of the middle-man is always risky. It's exactly the type of dirt that got me sent to juvenile detention at sixteen. I was young, stupid, and could never keep from getting caught to save my life. I used to think I was cursed or had some ungodly bout of bad luck and it's been that way ever since.

The job is risky. There are too many variables and opportunities for snags. The police could roust me. It's a busy corner, hand to hands in this city signal drugs to the cops.

And what if it is drugs? If I catch another charge, I'm gone for good. No matter what deal my lawyer could conjure up.

The businessman was nervous enough for the both of us. If I don't show, chances are he'll take the loss, lie low for a few days, and then go back into Dooney's looking for another sap to haggle with. But that could turn bad for Dooney, if the businessman keeps showing up every week and drawing attention to the shop. A bald fella like him, dressed in a thousand-dollar suit, surrounded by a sea of ex-cons wearing Salvation Army fits, stands out no matter how you cut it.

Every ounce of my being is telling me it's not worth it. It's telling me to leave town with the businessman's cash, hop a train or bus to Winston-Salem and then on to Mocksville until I reach the succor of my grandfather's farm. But I know that would only leave troubles here in Philly, like lighting a fuse on a powder keg and disappearing before it blows, and if Dooney got caught up in the aftermath, I couldn't live with myself.

I finish off the free whiskey and place the glass on the bar with finality. My lids are getting heavy, and I should start looking for a place to bed down. I glance at the clock hanging over the manikin.

"Got some place to be?" asks Earl.

"Know of any good hotels?"

"There's one on Walnut with discount rooms. They're doing construction."

"Doesn't sound too bad."

"If you don't mind the paint fumes."

I dig into my pocket and tip him three bucks, laying the singles on the table and then sliding them forward.

"I've got some peppermints and swisher cigars if you wanna cover up the liquor. . . ."

"It's fine. I'm walking tonight."

"Suit yourself."

I ease off the barstool, take a cigarette from my pocket, and bring it to my lips.

"I could use a light."

Earl brings his flicker to the tip of my cigarette and I take a steady drag until the smoke curls slowly out of my nostrils.

"Thank you," I say, as I exit the bar and reemerge into the night's warmth.

The Royale Hotel is a brick building—the type of place businessmen come to shack up with their women away from home—cheap and efficient and it has an Internet connection. In the lobby, caution tape blocks off the elevators. I take the stairs until I reach another lobby with a television, couch, and a table with a pot of coffee on it. I pass a small rack with brochures on things to do in and around Philly. One of the brochures has a photo of the Liberty Bell and a man dressed as Benjamin Franklin standing next to it, while another features city hall and art museums.

Philly has been putting lipstick and rouge on since I can remember—reinventing its decrepit streets like a Villanova debutante after plastic work. No one cares about the history. It's just a backdrop to a city on the brink of expiration. The jobs are slim. Mainly grunt work like collecting trash, driving a cab, or being a cop. The hospitals provide for those in the medical profession, and Philly has more lawyers than it knows what to do with. But it also has dope, lots of dope: Red tops, green tops, white tops, purple haze, stress, beasties, bomb, blueberry, orange kush, black tar, X, coke, and Lucy cigarettes can all be snatched up on the street with ease. The dope keeps the city from starving. But dope money brings the need for guns and the guns result in murders, and a high murder rate makes Philadelphia the third most dangerous city in the United States. But most people aren't losing any sleep over it. Everything about Philadelphia is crooked and fouled up: the mayor, a black man who supposedly bribed his way to a passing grade on the bar exam; a city councilman who played queer in order to get the gay votes; a grease trucker who sold hog trough cuisine and then disappeared when a single mother died from eating a bacon, egg, and cheese hoagie. It's a blue-collar town, with a blue-collar way of killing you. It eats at you like time ate at this hotel, but no one's going to restore you once it's done. Once the city has its fill of you, it leaves you bone dry.

I approach the marble counter. A man with slick dark hair wears a tag on his chest that reads MANAGER. I tell him I need a room. The man turns his nose up and then asks how long I'll be staying. I tell him a few days.

"How will you be paying?" he asks.

"You accept cash?"

"Yes," he says snidely. "Cash is fine."

I pay him forty-five dollars and he slides me a long brass key with the number 207 engraved, along with a smaller key.

"This is for the complimentary safe. If you lose the key, you'll be charged. Hotel policy."

He leans over the counter, looking down at my feet where my duffle bag is resting.

"Traveling light, are we? Well, no matter. Just know we charge the full night's stay. No hourly rate and it's half-price because of the construction, which will end this Friday. After that the rooms go back to full price."

He hands me my receipt. I pick up my duffle bag and head toward the elevator.

"Sorry, it's out of order," he says, watching a black and white security monitor. "But the stairs are working fine."

The manager's attempt at being witty fails, and I leave him with an uncomfortable look on his face.

Room 207 is small and is furnished with a round mahogany table, two brown leather chairs, and a brass floor lamp with an emerald green shade. The wallpaper is tacky: a gold and blue flowered pattern. I realize nothing in the room matches and remodeling couldn't have come sooner. The complimentary safe is a gaudy metal cube sitting on a splintered pale oak dresser. Next to the safe is a phone book. I take a seat on the queen-sized bed dressed in a mustard yellow duvet with matching pillowcases. I flip through the white pages for the businessman's name, but the search yields nothing. I guess the name Harlin is even less common than I thought. I dial the phone number on his business card, but get a voicemail with no greeting. Mr. Washington is in the business of hiding, and again I question what I've gotten myself into.

I go into the bathroom, splash my face with water, and dab it dry with a towel. I place my duffle bag on the bed and start unpacking my dress shirts. I hang a few shirts and slacks in the closet. There's a tap on the window, followed by several more. I walk over to the glass, lift the shade, and stare at the skyline. There's a dark gray mass of clouds filtering the moonlight, casting purple and blue hues. It had begun to rain, coming down in sheets. I open the window to let in the rain's scent. I inhale it slowly like a fine perfume, and then I collapse onto the bed.

I rest for an hour, half-asleep, half-awake. The rain: nature's tap dancer who doesn't know when to quit. The constant tapping on the window is giving me a pulsing headache.

I give up on sleep and prop the pillow up behind my head so I can face the window and watch the water stream down the glass. No matter how much I try to focus on the mundane, the businessman's proposition is robbing me of peace of mind.

I take a bath with some complimentary soaking salts intended to relax tension. They don't work. I towel off and throw on a pair of fresh boxers and a T-shirt. I remove a plastic laundry bag from the dresser and put in my soiled shirt. I dig into the pockets of my work pants and take out my change from the day's purchases. The paper with Marcus' phone number jotted on it floats to the floor. I bend over and pick it up with my fingertips clenched on its corners. Marcus was sitting under my nose the whole time. I'll dish him the job—send him in my place. He can make the delivery and pocket the five hundred. After all, he does have a baby on the way and the money will do him some good.

I pick up the phone and dial the number. An older woman with a smoker's hack answers and says she doesn't know any Marcus. I realize that I've dialed wrong. I replace the nine with a seven and dial again. There are four steady rings and then he answers:

"Yeah?"

"It's Paul from the shop," I say.

"I thought you would be a memory by now. What you still hanging around the city for?"

"It's not for nothing. I've got a job I'm willing to pass onto you. How about you meet me at the Royale Hotel? It's room 207, tomorrow morning. Say ten o' clock?"

There's a long silence and then Marcus breaks into laughter.

"So the suit did hit you off with a job and what now? You can't take it on account of your sweetie at the crib finding out you've been moonlighting with the cons? She called your probation officer, didn't she?"

"You sure got a pair of eyes on you."

"A blind man could see it coming."

I let him enjoy his assumption. I'll be off probation in a

little less than seventy-two hours and I still have to remind myself to do my weekly check-in. It's been a constant thorn in my side. Maybe Tammy was right. Maybe I was just biding my time with her until real freedom came.

My probation officer, Dougie Church, is a high school football star who lost his full ride to Temple University when his knee blew out. Besides being my probation officer, he's a friend, or the closest thing I have to one, and even then, I can't trust him—not completely. In a city like Philadelphia, a man needs all the friends he can get as long as he knows where he stands. Dougie once told me forty-two percent of the people murdered in Philly at one time considered their murderers close friends or associates—friendships that went back fifteen years. In this city, chances are you're going to know the bastard who's going to kill you—you probably grew up together on the same block: drank together, got high together, and broke bread together—making the killing intimate, personal.

I let Marcus ramble on before shortening the conversation with a couple of yawns. I reiterate ten o' clock. Then say goodbye and let him trail off as I place the receiver back on its base. I spend the rest of the night sleeping soundly.

CHAPTER FOUR

I WAKE AT SIX-THIRTY to the pounding of a jackhammer. I take a hot bath and put on a pair of khaki work pants, along with a white V-neck T-shirt and my boots. I head to the lobby hoping to find a decent continental breakfast. Instead, I'm welcomed by the hotel manager and a makeshift buffet table with a pot of cold decaf, three stale croissants, tiny boxes of cereal with no milk, and a few picked-over grapes sitting on it.

"You might want to head down earlier next time," says the manager, smirking and satisfied that I missed breakfast.

I step out into the early morning light. The battered leaves are dangling from the trees. The sun is reflected in rain-filled potholes, and it takes my eyes a second to adjust to the crystal glare. I walk toward Broad Street, passing the morning commuters with coffee mugs and briefcases in hand. I envy them. They walk with purpose. They've discovered their calling. Even if it's a nine-to-five block with a slave-driving boss, they're still expected every morning and people are counting on them.

I smile at a woman wearing a gray business suit and white blouse. She makes eye contact, but quickly looks away as if she's ashamed of taking the time to acknowledge me.

I get a cup of black coffee and an apple fritter from a chain coffee shop. I put a dollar-fifty into the tip jar, not because the service is so great, but because the barista has deep hazel eyes and a cute smile with a slight overbite that makes me feel like I owe her for being pretty. I have some time to kill before meeting with Marcus, so I take a stroll down South Street until I get to the docks. The boats are just coming into harbor, and I take a seat on a wet park bench. I toss a few crumbs of my apple fritter to the pigeons. They flutter and fight over them, pecking at each other and leaving not a morsel for the flies.

I wonder how much of Philadelphia a man can miss. The city is like an abusive parent that you hate to love and struggle to hate at the same time. Sometimes I want to shake sense into those people who rap about city pride and pass out pamphlets on saving historical monuments, or some electoral candidate that promises more of the same. What good is trying to save anything in this city? If the Liberty Bell were to shatter tomorrow they would sweep up the thousands of little pieces and move on. If the Benjamin Franklin lookalike finally keeled over, he would die broke and forgotten after two weeks. Philadelphia is a historic ghost town inhabited by those who don't know they're dead. In the past, runaway slaves died trying to get here. Now, I'm dying to get out.

I walk into the Free Library, brushing past a bum begging for change at the entrance. When I don't give him any money, he calls me an Uncle Tom and spits at my feet. I pretend not to notice, which only agitates him more.

I browse the net for the cheapest way to get back to North Carolina. A one-way ticket on a small airline will run me one hundred and sixty dollars, but I'll have a two-hour delay. I'm no good on planes. The last time Tammy and I flew, I came down with the worst cold from breathing in the recycled air. And I always end up sitting next to the most talkative passenger who gets offended when I end up dozing off mid-conversation.

The train is a little cheaper than flying, but it will take me as far as Greensboro, an hour away from my grandfather's farm. That far from the farm, I'd have to take a bus anyway and there are only two charters that leave in a day. I could end up stranded in Greensboro, depending on when the train got in. I figure the bus is the best bet. I can sleep and not have to worry about having to get off or missing luggage. It'll take me directly to Mocksville, trouble-free. The bus line website gives me an estimated ticket cost: twenty dollars more than the airline, which I find strangely amusing, but figure it has something to do with fuel prices or people being too terror cautious to fly.

A librarian points at my coffee cup and tells me I can't have food or drink near the computers. Content with the information I gathered from the internet, I brush her off and leave. I'll need to purchase my bus ticket soon, to insure the price doesn't go up.

I'm half a block away from the Royale when I see Marcus sitting on the steps, smoking. He's dressed in faded baggy jeans, white sneakers, and a bright orange basketball jersey.

"You're early," I say.

"I thought we could get this cracking sooner. I have some business to tend to with my baby's mother."

Marcus follows me up the stretch of stairs in silence until

we get to the lobby. The manager takes a long distasteful look at him.

"Who pissed in his cornflakes?" Marcus asks.

I tell Marcus not to mind him and we keep walking. Inside room 207, Marcus takes a seat in the chair.

"So what's the deal?" he asks.

"How do you feel about making five hundred cash?" I ask.

"How do I feel about it? What's the catch?"

I have a seat on the bed and take a sip of coffee before answering him. Marcus is playing like he's snug, but his constant knee jerk is giving him away. He's nervous.

"You trying to hustle me?" he asks.

"I wouldn't dream of it. I'm just trying to share the wealth."

Marcus' own words against him. He's stuck and if he backs out now he knows I'll think him coward.

"What do I have to do?" he asks.

"All you have to do is pick something up and deliver it. It's as simple as that."

"What is it?"

"I don't know, but I can tell you what it isn't. It's not dope or steel."

"How can you be sure?" he asks.

"You just have to trust me," I say.

Marcus studies me, his dark eyes searching my face, looking for a twitch, a sweat bead, anything that'll give away the hustle. I take another sip of my coffee, this time a longer, more confident sip than before.

"Fine, tell me where to go," he says.

I tell Marcus the place and the time: The corner of 15th and Pine Street, 12:30, tonight. Marcus gets to his feet and pulls up his sagging jeans. He sticks out his hand and we shake. Marcus digs into his pocket and comes out with a menthol cigarette and lights it with a plastic green lighter.

"Want one?" he asks.

"No thanks, but I could use the flame," I say. I take a cigarette from my pack and put it in my mouth. Marcus brings the fire to the tip.

"You know, these only run about ninety-nine cents," he says.

"I'm trying to cut back. If I don't have fire, I don't smoke."

"Why not stop buying smokes altogether and bum? That'll make you cut back."

"Something about having them in my pocket, knowing I can smoke one if I want. It's just better than not having them at all."

"As long as you can find a light," he says.

"*As long as I can find a light*," I say, poking fun at my own reasoning.

Marcus heads out, fanning his jersey that's dampened with sweat. I smoke my cigarette slow and take a few more sips of my coffee before getting up and watching Marcus head south on Walnut from the window. I spend most of the afternoon in the hotel room thinking about my life in the city and particularly about my life with Tammy. When night falls, I pick up a hoagie at a corner bodega and turn in early—a little after nine o'clock.

The next morning I pass on the hotel's continental breakfast and decide to take a walk through the Italian Market. It's my last day in Philly so I figure I'll take in the sights one last time. The market is busy as usual. I browse for about twenty minutes, leafing through the postcards and purchasing some Italian spiced jerky for the long bus ride. I stop in at Sabrina's on Catherine. I remember reading a favorable review in the *Philadelphia Weekly*, and I figure it'll make for a good last meal.

It's a quaint restaurant with a great stuffed French toast

combo and chicory coffee. It's one of those vegetarian friendly places that serve a good egg substitute. I like the ambiance. It's the type of restaurant a man can read his newspaper in peace without some obnoxious guy stirring up conversation about politics, sports, or women. Or maybe I just don't get out enough?

After breakfast I use a pay phone to call Dougie Church for my final check-in. He gives me some stern advice about keeping out of trouble. I tell him I have every intention of keeping my nose clean and that he shouldn't worry about me. He wishes me good luck and I hang up.

I walk to Love Park and sit a while looking through a weekly trade and people-watching. I turn to the employment section of the classified ads. There isn't much offered, just a few grunt jobs like street-cleaning and working as security. After reading I feel even better about my decision to pocket the businessman's cash and push the job off on Marcus. The sun dips behind the clouds, and I watch the shadow play on the buildings. I still appreciate the subtle beauty and peaceful moments the city does offer. Though they are few and far between, it's amnesty from the otherwise hour-to-hour madness.

I relax until a group of skateboarders show up, performing tricks and blasting music from a boom box. I watch the spectacle for a moment and then walk over to Dooney's Barber Shop to say goodbye. As I cross the street, I notice the closed sign in the window. Dooney is pulling the metal gate across the shop door. He's dressed in a black suit and a matching black and gray-striped tie. I've never seen Dooney dressed up before. He's sharp and his dress loafers look professionally shined.

"Closing early today?" I ask. "Got a hot date?"

Dooney looks up, somewhat startled.

"I wish," he says in a somber tone.

I get a better look at Dooney. It looks like he hasn't slept in days. His eyes are bloodshot and puffy.

"What's going on?" I ask.

"Somebody killed Marcus. They found him laid up in his car, parked on Front Street with a belly full of daylight."

"What?"

"I'm on my way to his girl's house now."

"Was it a robbery?" I ask.

"They're not sure, but they're trying to tie it to Osiris Jones and an old beef. I think it's some bullshit. Marcus may have been a knucklehead, but he was trying. If I find out who popped him, I'm going to . . ."

I rest my hand on Dooney's shoulder and he eases up some. He double-checks the lock, giving it a strong tug.

"Now that poor girl's going to have a dead man's kid. I tell you, Paul, I'm tired of this, sick and tired. And the cops aren't going to do a damn thing except bury it. Another nigger dead is how it'll play."

"You think Osiris is innocent?"

"The Osiris Jones beef has been over. He and Marcus squashed it. He wouldn't start shit with him now."

Dooney looks at his watch. "Sorry, kid, I have to cut this short. Come by the shop next week and we'll talk. Maybe you can finally get that mess you call hair cut."

"Actually, Dooney, I'm leaving tonight, taking the bus back to North Carolina."

"Ah, Youngblood, damn, I wish I would've known. . . ."

"I just wanted to come and say goodbye."

I embrace Dooney, his arm warm across my back.

"Hey, I've got something for you," he says, digging into his pocket. He pulls out a stack of bills tied together with rubber bands.

"What is this?" I ask.

"It's something to help you get back on your feet. A new start."

"You don't have to do that, Dooney. Besides, I thought you said you were struggling too."

"I know, but God's blessed me with some cash. He put it on my heart to help you out, and I can't argue with God. They say he works in mysterious ways."

"Mysterious ways?"

"Yeah, you know? Like God's little miracles. His way of smiling down."

I put a few bills in my pocket: two fifties and a couple of tens. The rest I shove into my duffle bag. I'm not sure how much Dooney gives me, but it feels like a couple of hundred. Dooney has no idea how the money is going to help. Now the world doesn't seem so heavy.

"Thank you," I say.

We hug again. Dooney releases me and straightens his suit coat, brushing out the wrinkles with his hands.

"You take care of yourself," I say.

"I'm gonna try," he says, his eyes red and seared with grief.

Dooney shoves his hands into his pockets and shuffles away, his head hanging low—defeated. He doesn't seem fit to be alone. I watch him take tiny awkward steps to the corner and then disappear around a building. I pause for a moment. I want to leave the city, but after seeing Dooney I'm conflicted. His grief is palpable and his hug left my heart heavy. Marcus was his friend and, like me, the son he never had. It isn't right to leave him like this, not after what he's done for me. I owe him.

I run down the block and round the corner after him. I see him in the distance, about a block away. I shout to him. At first he keeps walking, not missing a beat. Then, he stutter-steps and turns around to face me. I catch up to him tired and out of breath.

"Are you all right?" Dooney asks.

"I want to tag along."

"You?"

"Yes. If you think it'll be all right?"

"What about your bus? Won't you miss it?"

"No. It leaves late tonight."

"And you're sure?"

"I am."

"Okay."

I walk with Dooney another block to his car, a black Lincoln sedan with tan leather and cherry wood interior. Dooney slides in on the leather seat. I walk around the car to the passenger side and get in. His steering wheel is wrapped in a black plastic covering with tiny gripping beads. He puts his hands around the wheel, moving his fingers up and down like an exercise. Then he adjusts his side view mirror. It had been tilted inward to avoid being struck by a passing car or biker on the narrow street. I wait patiently as he toggles with a pad of buttons near the steering wheel, moving the mirror a little at a time until its perfect. When the task is complete, he pulls from the curb with a grunt.

"Are you comfortable?" he asks. "Not used to people riding with me."

"I'm fine. Don't be offended if I doze off. I get sleepy in cars."

"Don't worry, none taken."

Dooney tunes the radio to a classic soul station and I rest my eyes.

Maybe coming with Dooney will shine more light on what happened to Marcus, and maybe his girlfriend will know more details about his death. For all I know, I put him in front of the gun. I tell myself Marcus knew the risks when he took the job, he called himself schooling me to the streets. I was sure he could handle it. But if he knew so much, then why is he dead? Someone cut him down, a man I spent time with. They killed him and left his dead eyes to reflect a harbor he'll never see again.

I follow Dooney to the front door. He rings the doorbell and the door slowly opens revealing a young woman in her mid-twenties. Her skin is dark brown with a baby oil sheen, and her eyebrows are waxed pencil thin and don't quite compliment her face. Her beauty is hidden behind a thick layer of make-up, which makes her face look plastic and artificial. She would be halfway stunning if she weren't so hard. Every part of her looks like it's been touched by suffering. Even her eyes hold a considerable amount of pain.

Dooney wraps his arms around her and holds her close to his chest. I respect the moment and take a step back from the stoop to give them some privacy. I wonder if coming to the home of Marcus' girlfriend was a good idea. What if whoever killed Marcus was actually gunning for me?

"Shaina, this is Paul," Dooney says, while summoning me forward with his hand.

I shake Shaina's hand—it's small, dainty, and gets swallowed up in my palm. I can tell she's been crying for some time. Every nook and cranny of her face holds the residue of tears.

We enter the house. The shades are closed, and all the furniture is covered in dirty yellow plastic. There's an older woman, with long golden braids, dressed in an old-fashioned housecoat. Her legs are riddled with elephant veins and slight patches of discoloration—she doesn't look well.

The very pregnant Shaina braces her hand against her lower back and then plops down next to her. Dooney takes a seat in a gray leather recliner and I continue to stand.

He attempts to introduce me to the older woman, but she doesn't respond when he acknowledges her. Her eyes glazed over and vacant.

"Mama has been like this all day since we told her," Shaina says. "She just sits there all frozen and still."

"Shaina, I'm so sorry," Dooney says.

"I know Dooney. You coming here do mean a lot. Marcus really loved you."

I want to ask her about Marcus and if he spoke of any last-minute hustle, or five hundred dollars that was coming to him, but I can't muster the courage. To talk about Marcus' shady dealings would shatter the house of mourning. It's easier to mourn a man when you believe his nature was essentially good. The truth is Marcus was a hustler, a disciple of the streets. But what was the businessman, an undercover, a kingpin? Had he been playing me all along, only hooking me to off me later? Did Marcus try and take off with whatever was in that package? Could he have been that big of a fool? Or did they plug him when they realized he wasn't me?

"Have a seat, Paul," Shaina says. "You're making me nervous standing like that."

I take a seat on a vinyl stool in the corner, bracing my back against the wall for support.

"Did you know Marcus?" Shaina asks.

"I did, just not very well. We had just met."

"I see. Well, you probably got a good taste of him. It's only after you've known him for a while that he starts to wear on you." Shaina chuckles uncomfortably, and I regret she felt the need to break the silence.

"Ya'll want anything to drink?" she asks.

"No thanks," I say. "I'm fine."

"I'll take a soda," Dooney says.

"There's none in the fridge, but there's a case in the

basement," she says.

Dooney gets up and heads down the hallway to the basement steps. I wait until the sound of his heavy feet against the wooden stairs subsides.

"Shaina," I say, "I don't mean to pry, but did Marcus say what he was doing the night he was killed?"

"Not really. He said he had to step out for a while and that he would be back in about an hour."

"Did he take anything with him?"

"What? Like his piece?"

She smiles strangely.

"Please, I know what Marcus did. It's no surprise he ended this way."

Dooney pounds up the stairs with a case of cola.

"Just put it in the fridge," she says. "Thank you."

Dooney bumps around in the kitchen, stacking the cans in the fridge.

The doorbell rings and I obey my instinct to get up, but Shaina signals for me to stay seated.

"Probably just more family," she says.

She looks through the peephole and then opens the door slowly.

"What do you want?" she asks.

I'd know Osiris Jones' voice anywhere. It's soft with a permanent hoarse in his throat, and his words end in a whistle due to his chipped tooth, cutting through the air, giving him an uncanny lisp.

Osiris is bold, but bold enough to come to the door of the girlfriend of a man he's rumored to have killed? Things are beginning not to fit.

I can't make out what Osiris is saying, but Shaina tells him to stay outside and I figure he was pushing to come in.

I've laid eyes on Osiris before. I've been within inches of

him. I've smelt his aroma of Bogie cigars and sandalwood oil. One night we shared a holding cell. I had drank myself into a stupor and caused a ruckus outside of Morton's Jazz Cafe. The cops shuttled me to jail so I could cool off. The cell was relatively empty. All except a few hobos and a man dressed in a sleek black suit: Osiris Jones. Another man that he called Bear was standing guard over him. Bear was massive, a coal-black gargantuan with purple and black knuckles, no doubt bruised from the night's brawl. They sat for about fifteen minutes, Osiris with his legs crossed, his face absent of all emotion. He checked his watch repeatedly and sighed like jail was a nuisance, keeping him from an important engagement. Then he took a shine to me—asked me my name, where I was from, and who I worked for. I refused to answer all his questions except one.

"Paul Little," I said.

"Little Paul," Osiris retorted, followed by a baleful laugh.

He asked again where I was from. This time I answered, believing it was the best way to keep things polite. Not to mention, Bear was giving me an icy stare that made the hairs on the back of my neck reach for heaven.

"Here and down south," I said.

"Ah, yes," Osiris said. "God's country they call it. It's pretty down there. Good food, but hot, too hot and humid for me." He fanned his face with his hand, as if reliving a warm southern day.

The bailiff called Osiris' name and then opened the holding cell.

"It took you long enough," he said. "I was beginning to think you all were crazy enough to keep me in here overnight."

"No, Mr. Jones. It's just a formality. All charges have been dropped."

"Good," Osiris said, walking out with Bear in toe. "Bear

is getting hungry and he gets testy when he's hungry." He paused for a moment and then muttered something in the bailiff's ear. About ten minutes after Osiris left, the bailiff released me.

"Osiris said you and him go quite a ways back," the bailiff said.

"He did?" I asked.

"That's right. He said you were sober. So I'm letting you out."

"He decides who gets out around here?" I asked.

"He does tonight," he said.

"Okay," I said, still slurring.

That night, walking home I mulled over why Osiris helped get me out of the "drunk tank" early. When I got to my apartment, the thought vanished from my mind and I passed out, missing work and getting fired the next day.

Over time, Osiris grew to critical status. The police gave up trying to pin murders on him after he used a fast-food joint as his own personal slaughterhouse. He had tired of gunplay and decided to poison his enemies by having a cook who owed him money serve up arsenic-laced chicken and burgers at the local Crown Food. He was a cheetah and the rest of us gazelles. It was survival of the fittest. As far as the Philadelphia Police Department was concerned, if you crossed him then it was hell on you.

I struggle to hear Shaina and Osiris, but I can't make out their words. Sometimes their voices peak, but an argument never ensues. Dooney stays in the kitchen and out of sight, but I know he's privy to the scene that's unfolding in the doorway. I decide to get up and walk past the door to make my presence known. I'm not sure if it's the best move. But if Osiris knows there are men in the house, hopefully he'll keep the peace. I exchange glances with him. He looks like he's spent all night in a hot box without sleep. He's alone, which is out of character for him; he is always with Bear or at least one brutish brother in an expensive suit. Perhaps Bear is in the van parked out front, and given Shaina's pregnant condition, he didn't want to scare her.

They talk for about five minutes more, and then Shaina shuts the door, dead-bolting it behind her.

"Is everything all right?" Dooney asks.

"Yes, just fine. That fool has some nerve coming here. He's claiming he didn't kill Marcus. I mean swearing up and down that he's innocent. It's just crazy talk. If that man ain't sin, I don't know who is."

My stomach drops, and my tiny bit of hope that Osiris had developed a conscience overnight and had come to confess drops with it.

I dig into my pocket and take out a wad of bills and hand them to Shaina.

"I owed Marcus this."

"You owed him?" Shaina asks in an off-kilter tone.

"That's right," I say, assuring her.

"I thought you didn't know him that well?"

"I didn't, but he gave me a ride and spotted me some cash."

Dooney gives me a puzzled look.

"Paul, are you all right?" he asks.

"Honey," she says, "Marcus owes people. People don't owe him."

"Please, just take it," I say.

Shaina studies me and then takes the crumpled bills from my hand.

"I guess if you owed it to him," she says, her voice wavering.

"Sorry for your loss. I need to go."

I fumble with the lock, finally unlatch it, and then dart out of the front door, leaving Dooney in the kitchen dumbfounded. I sprint down the block until I see a cab barreling toward me and I hail it.

I have the cab drop me off at the Royale. Outside, a young girl, fair-skinned black, maybe Dominican, tries to hustle me for change. I quickly brush her off and head up to my room, passing the manager, who's delighted when I tell him I'm checking out. After throwing a few loose pieces of clothing into my duffle bag, I count up my money, making sure I have enough for my one-way ticket back to the South. I was so eager to get the hell out of that house that I didn't check to see how much money I pushed off on Shaina. To my dismay, I gave her all the cash I had in my pocket, making my penance a total one hundred and fifty dollars. I try to take solace in the fact that she's pregnant, and with Dooney's money I still have enough for my bus ticket, but that extra money could have come in handy with food and expenses. It's a setback, but I know if I don't get the hell out of town, the money might buy me a casket.

I pay the manager what I owe. He takes about five minutes counting up the cash, stopping, and then starting over twice. Then he remarks on how much the room would have been if it weren't for the construction. I grip the edge of the counter believing if my hands are occupied they won't go upside his head. He stutters a few words and then slides me a receipt under a complimentary chocolate with *thank you* written on the wrapper.

Outside the air feels a few degrees cooler now that the sun is low to the skyline. A taxi a block away is heading in my direction. I hail it. It pulls alongside the curb and I can see two women in the back seat. They get out of the cab holding stuffed shopping bags. One of the women, slightly plump wearing an expensive linen suit, tells me in a thick New York accent that it must be my lucky day. They were planning to get off at the next block. I play nice and smile, trying to hide my increasingly sullen disposition. I signal to the cabbie to pop the trunk and he does. I toss my duffle bag in and slide across the musty stained fabric, slamming the door behind me.

"Where to?" asks the cabbie.

The cabby's name is two words I can't pronounce and his license photo looks like it was taken three days ago. The checkered shirt he's wearing in the photo and the shirt he's wearing now are identical. Right down to the black ink pen in his pocket and the ketchup stain on his collar.

"The Greyhound station," I say.

"Once we're out of the traffic, it is smooth sailing," he says.

The sentence slides off his tongue like hot butter, and I wonder how many times he utters it in a day.

"Was pretty hot today, wasn't it?" he asks.

I don't answer. I'm preoccupied with a shiny piece of metal on the floor of the cab. I reach down and pick up a small black pocketbook with a chrome buckle. The purse is obviously left behind by one of the women in the cab before me. I debate hoping out of the cab and running it down the street to them, but I don't. I kick it under the passenger's seat so it's out of sight. I can't do anything to jeopardize catching my bus.

We sit idle at the red light. There's a line of cars ahead of us. The cabbie makes another attempt at small talk, but the scowl on my face repels every friendly advance. We start moving forward, slowly, inch by inch. People walk in front of the cab and against the light. The cabbie lays on the horn. A teenager with gelled spiky black hair and a jean jacket arrayed with political buttons walks in front of the cab and takes the brunt of the horn. He gives the cabbie the finger and kicks the cab door with his knee-high, red-laced combat boot.

"Asshole freak!" the cabbie shouts. "Can you believe that guy?"

The question is rhetorical and doesn't warrant an answer. We start moving again, this time at a steady pace. I try to relax some. I tell myself in an hour I'll be on a Greyhound bus, reclining in my seat and bidding farewell to Philly for good.

The cab picks up speed. I watch the fare meter climb. The cabbie notices me peering over the seat.

"Don't worry," he says. "It'll be a twenty-dollar flat fee."

"And if the fare is less than twenty?" I ask.

"Oh, it's never less than twenty. Sometimes it can be more. So I charge twenty. It's reasonable."

The cabbie uses this exchange as another opportunity for chitchat and starts asking me about my trip. He's so focused on me that he doesn't notice the girl who runs right into the path of the cab.

"Watch it!" I shout.

The cabbie slams on his brakes. They let out a squeal and then the odor of cooked brake dust. The girl presses her hands against the hood of the cab. Her hands are covered in dirt. At first she looks like a streetwalker who got too high for her own good, but my assumption is short-lived once I see her clothes. They're newly purchased styles—something a college student would wear: a white button-down blouse that's missing buttons, a ripped plaid vest, and a short denim skirt accompanied by a pair of tan wedges.

"Help me," she says, moving to my window and tapping the glass with her fist.

I study her close; she's been beaten and her nose looks

broken—the bone is poking out on the bridge resembling a camel's hump. Her pupils are reddish, the way I've seen in women of Creole heritage—her beady red coals darting every which way. And in a moment, I realize that I've seen her before, in fact; only moments ago, outside the hotel begging for change.

She frantically avoids being clipped by the sea of cars, jumping and reacting to every horn blow and shout. She reminds me of an infant in a bath for the first time, struggling to get its bearings while splashing to stay afloat—waiting for a strong arm to retrieve it from the basin.

The cabbie rolls down the window to ensure the girl can hear his shouts clearly.

"Get the hell out of the street!"

The girl continues to tap on my window, and the cabbie starts slamming his palms against the wheel.

"Please, take me to the hospital," she says.

"Get the fuck away from the cab," he says.

I know I shouldn't get involved. It's a police matter. The cops will be by any minute to pick her up. Someone had to have dialed emergency. I turn away from her, trying to keep my eyes focused on the back of the cabbie's head, which is now jerking to the beat of his curses. But I can't. Every time I look at her swaying in the street, barely able to stand, her clothes filthy, I wonder how long she'll last before being struck down.

I don't know if it's the guilt, but I'm compelled to unlock the door. I know I shouldn't, but maybe had I given her a few bucks, she might not be in this mess. I open the door and pull the girl into the back seat. Cars continue to honk behind us, and the light is stale green. The cabbie missed two opportunities to hang a right onto 12th, and the drivers waiting to turn are heated.

"What the hell are you doing?" asks the cabbie.

I can barely hear him over the barrage of horns.

"Take her to the hospital," I demand.

The girl's clothes are stained with tiny specs of blood that have accumulated mostly on the back of her vest, and there are small shards of glass embedded in her blouse. She doesn't make eye contact with me, and she makes a tiny sniff, like she's trying to keep the blood from rushing out of her nostrils. She keeps her head tilted back with her palms braced against her knees. If she is a junkie, her blouse is covering up the track marks. I scan her legs. No marks, only a thin layer of dirt on her knees and shins. She's some mix of black, but her facial features are ambiguous. They could be more European, or even Latin like Tammy. Her hair is thick and curly, borderline nappy. Her fingernails are French-manicured and the once-white tips are chipped and discolored—a few nails splintered and broken.

"Are you nuts?" the cabbie says, protesting the obvious. "I don't want to have anything to do with this." Who would want to have anything to do with this? Part of my brain is still trying to rationalize why I let her in the cab in the first place. The other part is pulsing slogans like "What's done is done" and "You can't go back in time" while a small less-important chunk is imagining an alternate future where I got out of the cab and chased down the ladies with the forgotten pocketbook—receiving a healthy monetary reward for the deed.

"I'll pay you," I say.

"What?"

"I'll pay you. Just take her to Jefferson."

The cabbie stares at me in the rearview mirror and our eyes lock in contention.

"Fifty dollars," he says.

"What?"

The girl's head bobs forward, and I notice a gang of hair clumped together with moist dirt and blood. I lean in for a closer look. The clump is a sticky red mass the size of a baby's fist. The blood is beet-red, and there's a crusty congealed trail leading down the back of her neck, like hardened candle wax.

"What did they hit you with?" I ask.

"I don't know . . . a stone I think. . . ."

She slumps over toward the door. Her body is going limp.

"I'm tired," she says.

"You have a concussion," I say.

I pat her face some, trying to keep her awake.

"Don't go to sleep. Try to stay alert."

"No dead girl in my cab," the cabbie says, shouting and shaking his finger like he's reprimanding a child. "No dead girl!"

"She's not dead, you ass, but she isn't getting any better the longer we sit here."

"Fifty bucks and I take her or you get the hell out."

"She's hurt!"

"She's a junkie!"

It's a gridlock of words, and he isn't budging. Precious time is being wasted. If the girl sleeps, she could do serious damage to her brain, irreversible damage. I dig into my pocket and take out a fifty and throw it into the cabby's face.

"Now drive—damn it!"

The cab heads south and then takes a right turn onto a street north of Walnut. The gash in the back of her head seems to have clotted, but her eyes are getting heavy. I try to keep her conscious with conversation.

"What happened to you?" I ask.

"I was mugged . . . took my purse . . . everything."

Her body crashes into mine as the cab takes a sharp

corner. I take her by the shoulder and fight to keep her steady.

"Careful! I think her nose is broken." The cabbie mutters something under his breath and then gives it more gas. The girl looks up at me, her beady red coals taking in my face.

"Thank you," she mouths, before shutting her eyes for good.

I carry her into the hospital emergency room after telling the cabbie to wait. He's reluctant at first, but I assure him there's a fat tip in it. I'm only a few blocks from the bus station and I can still make my bus without having to wait another thirteen hours for the next charter going south.

A nurse approaches me pushing a wheelchair. She's a thin brunette with tiny round shoulders and wide eyes, like those of a porcelain doll. She smacks red chewing gum, and there's a constant loud clicking in her jaw. I lower the girl into the chair slowly.

"What's her name?" she asks.

"Don't know. She said she was mugged."

"Is she conscious?"

"Barely," I say.

"I'll take it from here," she says.

The nurse wheels the semi-conscious girl toward the double doors marked Emergency Room. The girl grabs hold of the nurse's arm. The nurse bends over, putting her ear to the girl's mouth. I turn to see the cabbie faithfully waiting for me. I begin to walk toward the sliding doors when someone grabs me from behind. I turn and face a security guard, older, with a nervous twitch, gripping a spray can of mace. His eyes are shielded behind orange-tinted specs, and he has a salt and pepper moustache that's overgrowing his upper lip. My first urge is to bat his hand away, but his thumb is on his mace trigger so tight that he's bound to spray me out of anxiety. I don't move and he pierces his lips to speak, his moustache whiskers brushing against his stained yellow teeth.

"Sir. . . ?"

CHAPTER FIVE

I SIT IN THE DOWNTOWN interrogation room for about forty minutes before Dougie Church and a man who introduces himself as Detective Tatum King comes in. Dougie's dreadlocks are pulled back into a ponytail. They've gotten longer since I saw him last. He's chewing on a toothpick, shifting it from one corner of his mouth to the other. Whatever he's pondering, I hope it has something to do with me walking out of this room. I glance at the clock. The seconds fly by, as the small window of time before my bus leaves the station steadily decreases. Tatum King watches me out of the corner of his eye. His face doesn't hide his disdain for me: the sharp crease above his brow, his blood a hearty stock that's been simmering too long, enriched with the atrocities of the street—the tears of nine-year-old rape victims, botched felony cases, murdered witnesses. Ingredients that'll keep a man's blood up, keep it boiling. He reminds me of detectives in old movies. The ones who roll their own cigarettes and pull flasks filled with bourbon from their desk drawers when cases start to get the better of them.

"I thought we had an agreement, Paul," Dougie says, disappointed.

"I don't know what you're talking about," I say.

"You never gave me any trouble on probation. Instead you wait till you're off to start acting a fool."

"Man, I don't know what the hell is going on. They detained me at the hospital and then some cops came and brought me here."

"That girl just made eighteen," King says. "Damn near a kid."

His words are crisp. If he weren't so accusatory, I wouldn't mind listening to him. I can tell he's educated, not one of those cops who pluck away at the keyboard with two index fingers resulting in a report full of misspellings and grammatical mistakes. His accent is Baltimore, a fish scale. The skin around his words gives them a stiffness that's both menacing and impressive. It's the type of accent that makes a man sound honest even when he's lying, like he's been working hard all day, too worn-out to tell a lie.

"I don't know a damn thing about that girl," I say.

King sighs and then shuffles his feet like he's kicking imaginary dust across the floor. He's a tall man with the body of a swimmer. His cream-colored suit and gold wristwatch look expensive. Both accentuate his high yellow skin tone that makes him look sunbathed and more fitted for a spread in a men's trend magazine than police work. King stops shuffling and gives another bothered sigh. He moves behind me so his voice hovers over my head and I'm forced to turn around and face him.

"Sounds like she knows about you," he says.

"What?" I ask.

"You beat her pretty bad, Paul," Dougie says. He takes a seat across from me and folds his hands on the table. He resembles a child at bedtime prayer, his fingers inner locked, and his eyes solemn.

"I never touched her, Dougie. You know me. I'm the one who brought her to the hospital."

"Guilt could have gotten to you," King says. "Are you a church-going man, Paul?"

I slam my fist down on the metal table, and King leans in closer, putting his arms around each side of my shoulders and gripping the edge of the table with his palms. This is just a game to him, a cop exercise, something he'll joke about in the bullpen and local drinking hole.

I can feel his hot breath on my neck. He whispers into my ear the way a woman would—the way Tammy did.

"You're lying," he says.

He's so close I could break his nose if I want. And I would if it meant shutting him up, if it meant getting his sour breath off of my skin and his voice out of my head. But it's what he wants, to keep me in a holding cell overnight and a hearing come morning. The charge: battery of a police officer.

"She says you laid hands on her something fierce," Dougie says.

"She's confused," I say. "It wasn't me. I tried to help her. I want to see her. You show me where she says I hurt her."

"Paul, I want to believe you," Dougie says. "I do. It's why I came down here. But why would she lie? What the hell for?"

"I don't know."

I glance at the clock. In two minutes my bus will pull away without me, my duffle bag in the trunk of a cab doing laps around the city. I've seen things like this snowball. I ask for a lawyer and I'm guilty. I don't ask for one and I'm stupid.

I lay my head down on the table and close my eyes.

"He's shutting down," says King.

"Give him some time," Dougie says. "We'll come back later."

Hours later, Dougie brings me a cup of coffee and a granola bar from the vending machine. He places it in front of me, but refuses me eye contact.

"Dougie, you know this isn't right," I say.

Dougie doesn't respond and leaves the room. The white-hot light overhead is making me sweat and I wonder how guilty I'm beginning to look. I tear the granola bar wrapper with my teeth and take a bite of the snack. I was beginning to get light-headed, and the odor of the precinct wasn't helping. It's something between a hospital and a basement office. It reminds me of the first time I was locked up in county. I did a six-month stint. I broke my grandfather's heart. He wrote to me once, expressing his disappointment. When I was released, I went to see him. He was in the late stages of dementia, and I took advantage of his failing memory. I convinced him that my jail time was a figment of his imagination and instead of lock-up, I was out of town on a business trip. It took two weeks for the false memory to completely take hold. When it did, he would ask me if my company was planning another trip and if I would bring him back a souvenir.

Tatum King opens the door and peeks in, checking on me like a child on time-out. He knows I'm innocent, but he also knows that I'm capable of what I'm being accused of. It's as if I'm being persecuted because at one point in my life I might have really harmed that girl. And in some ways, I'm as toxic as the man who did hurt her. For King, I may be innocent this time, but it doesn't mean three weeks down the line I won't be sitting in this same seat, guilty as sin.

Another hour passes securing the fact I've missed my bus. The girl has cost me my trip, my bag, and therefore my money.

Dougie Church enters the room with a frustrated look. The toothpick chewed and spent.

"We have to talk," he says.

"Get to talking then."

Dougie takes a seat across from me.

"There's been a mistake."

"Who you telling?"

"The girl is going to drop the charges. But King says it's best not to leave town for a few days."

"In case he's able to convince that girl I beat her? That's bullshit. I'm off probation. I'm leaving."

"It doesn't work that way," Dougie says. "I haven't officially turned in the paperwork. In this case, I get the final say on the matter."

"What?"

"That's right, Paul. I decide. I'm sure I could convince Judge Giovanni to extend it out another week or month. Just until we find out what really happened."

"You wouldn't."

"I would, Paul. I have, for two more days. If you're innocent, then you'll go about your business and all is right as rain."

I stand up and Dougie stays seated.

"Don't you go near her, Paul."

"Take a breather, Dougie. I don't want anything to do with the broad. Besides, where am I going to go? I've got no money."

"I've got a boss to answer to," he says, defensively.

"I'm no damn rapist or abuser. You know me better than that. You're just trying to look good for your cop pals."

Dougie lowers his head. I'm not sure if it's shame or if he's just tired of looking at me. I leave Dougie in the interrogation room and I take my time walking out. I head down the hallway at a turtle's pace, making sure Detective Tatum King gets a good look at my back as I exit through the station doors.

Outside, I get a whiff of cigarette smoke and I follow the trail to a group of cops, young bulls, corralled on the front steps. I walk over and ask for a light. Reluctantly, one of the cops hands me his lighter and I light my cigarette, until the cherry glows orange and tiny specs of ash take flight. I feel naked without my duffle bag and needless to say the money tucked away inside. Every time I think about it, my neck tightens up and sends a sharp pain to my temple. I'm back to square one, with barely enough for a sandwich or a soft pretzel. I thank God that it's not winter and then curse him for it in the same breath. I'd rather find some alley, get stoned and freeze to death by morning. Instead, it's seventy degrees, crystal clear, and I feel like walking.

I head toward Love Park, puffing away on my smoke and thinking about Tammy. I wish I knew a life with no regrets. But all I can see is collages of my faults and mishaps, and I'm beginning to think my life with Tammy could fit into both categories. I wanted to protect Tammy from what I know is still lurking inside me, but by doing so I also sealed my fate. Now Philly holds claim over my body like an undertaker and I can't even barter my soul to get out.

I'm thirteen blocks into my walk when I realize I'm nowhere near Love Park. I've walked right up to Tammy's brownstone steps. The smell of her cooking wafts through the open window—rice, adobe, and the sweet smell of plantains. I have good mind to go up there and beg her to take me back. She would hate me for hours, maybe days, but she would feed and clothe me. Tammy has always been a giver, a caretaker. There's something inside of her that kicks in the way a back-up generator does when the power fails. She can't stand back while someone is suffering and needy. It's probably why she went into nursing in the first place. When she used to work for Hospice, she would come home in tears and I knew someone she had gotten close to passed on. I never had the heart to tell her what I really thought. How could she let some stranger grow on her to the point she would be a wreck for days? She knew they were on their way out, but she had no filter, no protection—her heart was on her sleeve and she was wide open.

My cigarette burns to its filter, and I flick the butt toward the concrete. A breeze catches it and carries it to the bushes. I take a seat on the curb and rest for a moment. I contemplate my next move. I remember my grandfather saying he hitch-hiked from New York to North Carolina as a young man. But the world was different then. All he had to worry about was getting things thrown at him by brawly white boys and making sure he wasn't picked up as a vagrant. Who knows what would happen to me with my luck? Maybe a drunk driver would strike me. Or I'd be the victim of a freak hail-storm that knocks me out cold and wipes my mind clean. I'd wake up with amnesia. I could start over, be whomever I wanted.

A patrol car pulls up to the stop sign and shines its spot-light on me. I sit in defiance—eyes wide in the face of the blinding light. The officers laugh and then turn the light off. I pick up a small stone and skip it across the street. It bounces funny and then nails the police cruiser's door on the driver's side. The officer turns on his blue light and gets out with his hand on his baton.

"This is city property, asshole."

I smile at him and it seems to get under his skin. He hikes up his pants and then looks back at his partner, who hasn't gotten out of the patrol car.

"You hear me talking to you, buddy?" he asks.

The cop is overweight with a double chin. He reeks of sweat, and his hair is matted down from wearing his police visor all day. He walks toward me with a bowlegged strut and shoves his baton in my face. His skinnier partner gets out of the patrol car. He is wearing black sneakers instead of the standard boots. He too approaches me. He's younger and scrawny, with a military buzz cut and peach fuzz over his lip. The fat cop must be his training officer, and I rethink what I've done. He could easily make an example out of me for the young bull. As the skinny cop gets closer, I get a good look at his nametag. His name is Wilson and he's excited like a kid itching to pop his cherry with a few swings of his nightstick. It must be the most action he's had all night. I size them both up. They're the type of fellas that would be traded for a carton of cigarettes on the inside, nothing intimidating about them. If it weren't for their guns, I'd stomp their throats shut and drop them in North Philly for the dopers to have their way with. That's a part of the city that even the beast doesn't want a piece of.

"Are you a retard or something?" says Wilson. "The officer is talking to you."

"Get that baton out of my face," I say to the fat cop.

Wilson is taken aback and then looks toward his fat superior waiting for instructions on how to proceed. The fat cop puffs up, raises his baton, and wiggles his fingers around the handle.

"Take it easy," a voice shouts out from the darkness. I turn to see Dougie Church flashing his badge. His truck is parked in the alley next to Tammy's building. He walks with his badge high for the cops to see, and they slowly put their batons back into their holsters. Wilson strains his eyes trying to get a good look at Dougie's badge.

"Parole officer," Dougie says.

"He yours?" the fat cop asks.

"Yeah, what's the problem?" Dougie asks.

Dougie doesn't cower and gets right into the cop's face, and I decide he's redeemed for the way he treated me earlier. Dougie has always been nosy, but this time I'm grateful for it. I must have sparked his curiosity enough that he tailed me from the station.

"Nothing, this fella was just apologizing."

"For what?" Dougie asks.

The fat cop looks at me, squinting—his brow tight with fury.

He wants to hit me so bad he can taste it.

"Nothing, forget it," he says.

Wilson gives a disappointed sigh and takes two steps back, keeping his eyes on me, before finally turning and getting into the patrol car. The fat cop lets a curse word fly, shrugs his shoulders, and then gets in behind the wheel. He takes a sip from something shiny and I realize how bad things could have gotten. Dougie and I watch as they gun the engine and drive past with Wilson squeezing his trigger finger at me.

Dougie says: "Cops' blood is always on boil and the long hot days don't help. You add liquor into the mix and you've got a recipe for trouble."

"You were tailing me?" I say.

"It's my path home. What the hell were you thinking? You know they would have had their way with you without hesitating."

"At least a holding cell would give me four walls for the night."

"Why aren't you staying with Tammy?"

"It's a long story."

Dougie sighs and then clips his badge back onto his belt.

"You can crash at my place tonight," he says.

"You sure?" I ask.

"You can sleep on the sofa."

Dougie reaches down, and I take his hand. He helps me up and we head toward his truck. It's an old pick-up that smells of motor oil and stale coffee. He starts the engine and the thick smell of exhaust makes its way through the vents. He shifts into drive and we head down the alley. I strain for another look at Tammy's window and get a glimpse of her brown skin against white cotton as we drive past.

"Sorry about the interrogation, but I have to keep a good working relationship going with the cops. It's just a matter of playing along. Besides, King is dirty. You should be happy the girl dropped the charges, because with King, evidence has a funny way of just showing up."

"What about not turning in my parole release?"

"Relax. I'll turn it in first thing tomorrow morning."

"Good."

"So what's going on with you, Paul?" he asks. "You seem to be attracting nothing but heat tonight."

"I'm spent, Dougie. I was on my way out of town and I got held up at the police station on account of the girl. A cabbie took off with my duffle bag and all the money I had for the trip."

"And what of the girl?"

"It's like I told you, she was beaten when I found her. I took her to the hospital trying to help. Guess it backfired. Now my only hope for money is to come off a dice game with a fortune."

"You and I both know you've never had a hot hand," he says. "Don't throw your pennies in the well just yet. Maybe we can find the bag? I'll make some calls. If that doesn't work, I can set you up with something."

"I really need to get the hell out of town quick, Dougie."

"Cool your heels for a few days and we'll find a way to up your cash flow. Maybe you can clean the clinic again."

"Dougie, you know I burned that bridge long ago."

"Oh, that's right. Sorry."

I've said enough. I rest my head back and shut my eyes. Dougie stops with the questions.

Dougie's apartment is a cramped one-bedroom a few blocks north of Broad Street. I walk in, and my eyes go straight to his pride and joy, a big-screen television that he couldn't stop bragging about even months after he got it. There's a black leather couch that isn't space efficient but nice enough to impress a one-night stand, and the walls are covered with framed posters of professional football players and characters from gangster films. There's erotic African art depicting naked, oiled, bodies engaged in fantasy sex. It's the type of art I've seen sold outside of beauty shops and soul food restaurants. Some of the prints have neon green and pink ink that glows under black light, the way exotic dancers nail polish can in strip clubs.

It's not the type of place I ever envisioned Dougie living in. I'm not sure what I envisioned, but somehow Dougie's bachelor pad with dorm room décor makes sense. He's living out the college experience that was denied to him on account of his injury. And the more I look at the brass trophies and championship rings, the more I can't help but pity him. Dougie actually had a way out of Philly. He was good enough to play pro and smart enough to make the best of it. But rotten luck, God, or the city itself felt it fitting to keep him here.

Dougie takes a pillow and blanket from the hall closet

and tosses it on the couch.

"This should be good for you," he says.

"Thanks."

Dougie goes into the kitchen and takes out two bottles of cheap beer and twists the cap off before handing me one. It's refreshing going down, but has an aftertaste that's bitter and lingers in my throat too long. I must be dehydrated because I keep drinking until it's nearly gone.

"Easy, champ," Dougie says with a smirk. And before I know it, he's already positioned in front of me with another ice-cold beer still smoldering from the cap being popped.

"Have another," he says. "It'll help you sleep."

I finish off the beer and start on the fresh one. Dougie takes a seat across from me in a black recliner.

"I take it you've heard about Marcus?" he says. "The streets have been talking pretty loud."

"I heard."

"What do you think happened? I mean the bulls don't know anything and they're shaking down everybody south of 40th Street."

I let the beer pour down my throat and buy some time before answering.

"So . . . what you think?" he asks.

"Don't have an opinion really. Someone had a problem with him and solved it."

"No, it's more than that. I think this is big."

I don't know if it's the beer or Dougie talking about Marcus that's making my stomach churn. I wouldn't mind him running his mouth if he had information, but he's prying and I can barely keep my eyes open.

"You really haven't had your ears to the streets, Paul."

"I guess not."

I finish my beer, and Dougie takes my empty bottles and

heads into the kitchen. I prop the pillow behind my head and stretch out on the couch, putting the blanket over my legs.

"If it's all the same to you, Dougie, I think I'll get some sleep now."

"No problem. You get some rest and I'll see you in the morning. Don't you worry, Paul. Something tells me everything's going to work out real easy."

Dougie disappears into the black hallway that leads to his bedroom. I conjure up the vision of Tammy passing in front of the open window and play it over in my mind, until it lolls me to sleep.

I wake to the scent of expensive cologne and the cold steel tip of a gun barrel pressed against my nose. I open my eyes and the sunlight comes fast. It takes a moment for the haze to subside, but when it does the image of a wafer-thin man holding a thirty-eight is in front of me.

"Don't move," he says.

I nearly bite off the tip of my tongue. I've never had a gun in my face. I've had knives, bats—even a corkscrew once, but never a gun. I'm close to losing my composure.

"You know who I am?" he asks.

"Osiris," I say, my voice strained.

"Get up slowly," he says.

I do as I'm told, sliding the blanket off and advertising every movement so I don't spook him.

"Put your shoes on," he says, sliding my boots toward me.

"Where's Dougie?"

"He took a walk."

I finish tying my laces, and Osiris orders me out of the apartment, shoving his gun into my ribs. We enter a freight elevator I passed coming in, but assumed wasn't working. We ride it to the lower floor and then Osiris ushers me out the rear lobby exit.

Outside, Osiris slides open the door to an economy van parked in an alleyway next to Dougie's apartment building. The van is old and rusted—the paint a gray primmer. He orders me inside.

"Where are we going?" I ask. He's silent. I crawl into the musty van. It reeks of urine and stale malt liquor. Bottles—some broken and some capped at half-full—are thrown about. In the corner are a pair of spent panties and a collection of used condoms that have dried—the lubricant reduced to chalky powder. And there is a steel fence-like partition between the flatbed and the cabin.

"You're not going to be a problem, are you?" Osiris asks.

"Well, you're the one with the gun, aren't you?"

"I'm not going to kill you unless you give me good reason. I'm more interested in what you have to say for yourself."

"Is that right?" I ask.

"Yes," he says.

"So, what was wrong with Dougie's apartment?"

"My place is safer."

My eyes drift to the gun.

"Safer?" I say.

"That's right and don't bother with the door. It only opens from the outside."

Osiris slams the sliding door and gets in behind the wheel. He starts the engine and we head down the alley and then merge onto Catherine Street.

"Why did you do it?" he asks.

"Do what?"

"Kill Marcus," he says.

Osiris speeds up, taking a sharp curve and sending my body slamming into the side of the van. I grunt. The pain is so severe that for a moment I'm convinced my shoulder is knocked out of its socket.

"I didn't kill anybody. Why the hell would I kill him?"

"Who knows? Why does anyone kill anyone?"

Osiris jerks the wheel and then takes a sharp left into another alley. He's avoiding all major streets and he keeps looking in his side mirrors.

"I hope that's not what you snatched me up to discuss because you could have asked me that at Dougie's place. Saved us both the trouble."

"I'm trying to see where you fit in all this. Out of the blue you show up. Marcus gets killed. Shit doesn't add up. You don't look like a killer, but my gut tells me you know something."

"Well, your gut is wrong. I heard you pulled the trigger."

"I'm the easy fix—the scapegoat. But Marcus is one man I didn't kill. He used to come by on the weekends always looking for a job. Sometimes he would cop purple caps off me. He was a good customer. Why would I kill a good customer?"

"I never took Marcus for a doper."

"Not him," he says. "For his girl."

"Shaina?"

"No, the other one with the flowery name. Rose, Daisy, something like that."

"Doesn't catch."

"I look for him sometimes on the street, that damn jersey with Wallace on the back. I never wanted him dead. The beef we had wasn't worth killing over. But I ran my mouth on it just to let folks know I wasn't going soft. Now Moiye is on me. I can't sleep, can't eat, my business has frozen up. Every move I make I swear I'm being watched."

"Richard Moiye?" I ask.

"Philadelphia's finest, and I can't shake him. If there's a medal for being a scab, he has it."

Osiris slams his brakes for a red light and sends me sliding forward smacking my face against the steel partition. I see my moment to escape and quickly jerk the door handle, but the door doesn't open.

"Like I said, it only opens from the outside," Osiris says, pleased with himself and the van's rigged door.

I give a frustrated sigh.

"What the hell you want from me, man?" I ask.

"I just want the truth," he says.

"I told you the truth. Now where the hell is Dougie? Did you kill him?"

"What for?" Osiris asks, calmly, without taking his eyes off of the road.

"Then where is he?"

"Hell if I know. But he ain't dead."

I picture Dougie sitting pretty somewhere with a pocket full of cash courtesy of Osiris, and my well-being the furthest thing from his mind. I was seduced by the thought that he was my friend, or the closest thing to it. He was the only thing that linked me to the streets. I've worked hard to make myself a ghost. As far as the world was concerned, Paul Little was released from Curran-Fromhold one spring morning, hopped a bus, and disappeared. Even when someone would look at me with a faint familiarity, they wouldn't stare long. I made sure that the man who entered prison didn't look anything like the man who came out.

On the inside, we were only allowed a haircut every two weeks, so I bribed the C.O. in cigarettes and girly magazines, so he'd let me get a weekly cut. I had witnessed too many prison yard brawls that resulted in pretty brothers with dreadlocks, braids and Afros waking up in the infirmary, missing chunks of hair and scalp. Once I got out, I grew my hair into a natural. Tammy poked fun at me because I pampered it and trimmed it myself, so it stayed neat.

I'm an average-looking brother. No striking features, no hazel eyes, or something else out-of-the-norm for black men, just plain brown or chestnut, as Tammy liked to say. I've been told I have a pleasant face and I've always managed to garner a few glances from most women, but overall I'm nothing special. But now I'm the apple of Osiris' eye and if Dougie is breathing, I'm going to make him pay for my loss of anonymity.

We drive about twenty minutes more, until we reach Osiris' compound—an old apartment building off Front Street. A block from where Dooney said they found Marcus dead in his car.

The building needs to be torn down. The brick is bleached white from pigeon feces, and a resident homeless man is camped out on the front stoop. Osiris gives him a head nod and puts a few bucks in his cup.

"Anybody scoping the place today?" Osiris asks.

"A black Lincoln drove by a few times, but other than that everything is on the up-and-up," he says, showing missing teeth and blackened gums.

Inside, I follow Osiris across the dirty checkered marble floor of the lobby to an elevator. We ride to the second floor and walk to the end of the hallway. It takes him what feels like five minutes to unlatch every lock on his door, four deadbolts to be exact.

The loft is large with three partially draped bay windows that overlook the harbor. Everything is dusty and the windows look as if they haven't been opened in some time, which accounts for the stuffiness and foul odor. It smells like a locker room.

"This building is set to be restored," he says.

He takes a seat in a folding chair and gives a loud yawn

followed by a stretch of his arms. He looks like a prizefighter who has just lost a title bout. It's the first chance I've had to get a good look at him. He's been beaten, his eye swollen, and face clad with bruises. The swelling exaggerates Osiris' naturally high cheekbones, which make his eyes look slanted and sunken in. Osiris' lips are thin and his chin dimpled and long. His unusual look reminds me of a man I knew in prison who claimed he was the descendant of a Cherokee chief, but later recanted when confronted by a Mexican-Indian gang demanding he cough up proof.

"There's some Scotch in the kitchen," he says, keeping his pistol on me. "Make us some drinks. Glasses are in the liquor cabinet."

I go into the kitchen at the other side of the loft. A half bottle of Scotch is on the countertop. Empty bean cans lie in a heap around an aluminum garbage bin filled to capacity with water bottles, protein bar wrappers, and TV dinner boxes. I remove two tumblers from the cabinet and pour the dark liquor. With the gun's sight positioned at my head, carrying the glasses is no easy feat. My knees knock with unease. The Scotch swivels in the glasses, threatening to spill over the rim. I keep reminding myself, if Osiris wanted me dead, I'd be dead. But it's obvious there's something he needs me for. There's some reason he took the risk picking me up in the first place. By the time I reach Osiris, he's standing with his hand extended, ready to receive the glass, and the pistol is slightly lowered, pointed at my belly. I give him the healthier glass and after a few sips, he slips the gun into his waistband.

"I'm not interested in killing anyone," he says. "I'm just a businessman trying to get back on my feet."

The loft is bare, except for piles of books scattered about, which seems peculiar, but gives me hope that Osiris is a rational man.

Osiris' voice bounces off the walls and the indentations in the carpet tell me at one point it was fully furnished, and judging by his expensive glasses, I'm sure with quality.

"Where's your furniture?" I ask.

"It's all gone," he says.

"Seized?"

"Sold."

"Why?"

"I needed to pay a debt and it's still not completely paid up," he says, swallowing the rest of the Scotch and then slamming the glass down on the card table.

"What about Bear?" I ask. "He quit too?"

Osiris squints, and I realize he never told me about Bear.

"What did you just say?" he asks, pulling the gun from his waist and shoving it in my face. "You know Bear?"

"Not really. Just his name, you know street talk."

"The streets don't talk about Bear. He's nobody."

"It was a slip," I say. "I must have heard his name in passing or something."

Osiris points the pistol at me. He moves in close, putting the barrel to my throat.

"I know you," he says, studying me hard.

"No, you don't."

"I know you, damn it. Maybe years back. But I never forget a face."

"You're mistaken. Now, can you lose the gun?"

"No. I'm positive . . . wait, Little Paul," he says, his cold frown becoming a smirk.

Osiris finally lowers the gun and shoves it back into his waistband, where hopefully it will stay.

"Shit, man. I knew there was something familiar about you. I sprung you that night, had that chump guard let you out."

"Yeah, thanks for that."

"Well, shit. Small world."

"Real small."

"Times sure have changed since then. Bear is gone, disappeared when I couldn't pay him—so much for loyalty. The only thing I have left is my pigeon."

"Your pigeon?"

"Keep him on the roof. Pour me another and I'll introduce you to him."

Although birds have been known to make me itch, I don't want to give Osiris a reason to pull his gun again. I pour him more of the Scotch and then follow him to the roof access.

Osiris shuffles over to the empty pigeon cages that stretch from one end of the roof to the other. He removes a lone spotted pigeon. It's definitely not one of the everyday crumb snatchers you find in Love Park. It looks more like a dove than a pigeon.

Osiris takes a grape from his pocket and feeds it to the bird.

"They're smarter than most people think. I flip them, been doing it for years. I've built up a nice collection, but had to sell them to stay afloat. This is my last bird. You should have seen some of the birds I had. They were worth a couple of grand, hard to believe, I'm sure. Most people are trying to get rid of pigeons. Putting poison in birdbaths and feeders, spikes on building edges, all because somebody decided they were a problem, a nuisance."

"A couple of thousand, you say?"

"That's right. It broke my heart to see them go." He releases the bird into the air. The bird circles just above Osiris' head, before finding its way back to its cage.

"When I look at you, you know what I see?" he asks.

"No."

"I see a man just like that pigeon. You're just circling until you find your way back to a cage. And the only way that doesn't happen is you've got to have a plan. So what's your plan, Paul? Why the hell you walking these streets dressed like a garbage man?"

"I was jacked on my way out of town. I've got nothing except the clothes on my back."

"Jacked by who? A bum?"

"Not exactly."

"You're no killer. Not the kind that would put all them holes in Marcus. You just ain't got it in you. Which means somehow you got mixed up in this mess either on your own, or by someone else's hand. Either way, you're bound to be collateral damage when this thing blows up."

"It's looking that way."

"I think we could help each other."

"How?"

"I've got a job for you."

"Men who work for you either die or end up wishing they were dead."

"It's not like that. It's nothing dangerous. Besides, the way I see it, you owe me for that night in lock-up."

"How do you figure that?"

"I could have left you in that cell. And who knows, maybe one of those homos could have gotten to you."

"Bullshit."

"Look, you simple son-of-a-bitch, I've got a way to get you paid."

"Why the hell should I trust you?"

"I'm speaking the gospel here. The same way I sprung you from that cell. I can get you paid and then you can get out of town, or whatever it is you're trying to do."

I decide it's worth hearing him out. In addition to his

being likely to shoot me if I don't help him, I'm desperate for cash.

"I'm listening," I say.

"I'm a prisoner in this loft. I've got surveillance watching my every move and it's stopping me from collecting on a debt, a debt that would allow me to square all my other debts."

"I'm not a debt collector."

"You're right. A debt collector is a professional. I can't afford a professional. But you I could hire cheap. Take a look in the mirror. You look like you'd kill for pennies."

"So what if you're right? I don't want to get mixed up in anything."

"All I'm asking is for you to collect some money that's owed to me. You get paid and we go our separate ways."

"Who's the debtor?"

"Franklin Webster. He lives up in University City. A white boy with an attitude. He's got more brains than style and a slick mouth. It's nothing you can't handle, though."

"How much money are we talking?"

"He owes me twenty grand. You'll pocket a grand. Your cut ain't negotiable, so don't waste your breath."

"Like you said, I come cheap."

Osiris is too desperate to be blowing hot air, and a thousand dollars will make up for Dooney's lost charity and put me a thousand steps closer to North Carolina.

"What's Frank's address?" I ask.

"It's not that simple. He never sleeps in the same place, always moving around. He normally crashes at a handful of party spots where he moves his dope, or my dope, I should say. You'll have to sniff him out. Start with the college kids. Find a party or two, and you'll find Frank." Osiris takes a clove cigarette from his pocket and lights it.

"Fine. When do I start?"

"First, let's get you cleaned up. You look worse than an unmade bed."

After I shower, Osiris tells me that I have to maintain a particular image if I work for him. Osiris walks me into the bedroom he's sectioned off with dummy walls and directs me to a closet full of suits—custom fits of the best fabrics: Italians, double-breasted, and seersuckers. I button the blue silk shirt that matches the gray suit best. Osiris notices a small tattoo of a cross on my chest—crude and gothic, the end result of an ink pen and a sowing needle.

"You know the Lord?" he asks.

"I know he'll wait for me," I say.

Osiris doesn't seem as high-strung as he was earlier, which I attribute to the second or third glass of Scotch in his hand.

"It fit all right?"

"It'll do."

"What size loafer are you?"

"Ten and a half."

"I guess you're stuck with those boots. I don't want you stretching out my Italian leathers."

He studies the suit with a strange gleeful glow—the way a chef admires a painstaking meal he's prepared before turning it over to be devoured. I wonder what Tammy would say if she could see me? Clean-cut and fitted like a prince. It's what she always wanted, but I wouldn't submit. There is nothing royal about me. I'm the scum of the earth and in my past life I was most likely dirt, and a woman of flesh and blood doesn't deserve dirt.

"I remember when I bought that suit," he says. "It was at the Brooks Brothers on Walnut. I knew I made it then."

"It's a nice suit."

I'm able to get a closer look at some of the books. Some neatly stacked and some scattered— two or three lying in the corners of Osiris' bedroom; paperbacks, hardcovers, and some with no covers at all. Osiris notices me looking at the books.

"You read?" he asks.

"Yes."

"I never found an appreciation for it until prison. I can't watch television. I used to keep one for entertaining and because it looked good. But it kind of hurts my head. Reading keeps my mind sharp."

"That's a good thing."

I get a good look at the titles. There are books on agriculture, the Civil War, an old copy of *War and Peace*, slave poems, true crime, and detective fiction, a section dedicated to folklore, mythology, and religion.

I remove a paperback with a solid black cover from his stack.

"Can I borrow this?" I ask, holding it up for him to see.

"You want to read that?" he says. "It's a textbook they had us read in prison. I was the only guy to understand some of it."

"I read anything I can get my hands on," I say.

"Sure, take it then."

I place the book in my suit pocket.

"I want you to take this, also," he says, handing me a small cell phone.

"Why?"

"So I can call you and check on things. It's a throw-away. When the minutes die, toss it. But make it last until you get me my money."

He removes another device the length of a ballpoint pen from his pocket. It's black with a few buttons down the side.

"What is that?" I ask.

"GPS. It's linked to my cell phone. Tracks every move you make. It was costly, but worth every cent."

"I won't need that."

"Sorry, friend. It's not an option. It's the only way I'll be able to keep tabs on you. The range expands the city and well into South Jersey. Not that you should be in Jersey—unless Frank takes a vacation."

I slip the phone and the GPS tracker into my jacket pocket.

"If you like, I can give you a piece. Any particular caliber?" he asks.

"A gun won't be necessary."

"Why not? It's the type of message Frank will understand quickly."

"Keep it. I don't like guns."

"And you've lasted this long in this city? You some kind of monk?"

I cut my eyes at him.

"Suit yourself. Have another drink and then you should be on your way."

"I'll do without the drink."

"Hell, you are a monk," Osiris mutters under his breath.

CHAPTER SIX

OSIRIS OPENS THE LOBBY DOOR of his building and takes a quick look around. Before I walk out, he slips me two hundred dollars.

"It's all I can spare," he says. "You can use it for cabs, food, and bribe money. You probably should get something to eat and then get to work."

I shove the money into my right slacks pocket.

"Remember to keep that phone on," he says. "I'll be checking in on you."

Osiris shuts the door and I walk down the steps and to the sidewalk, headed toward Passyunk. The suit fits snug, and with every step it gives a little. By day's end, it'll be wearing me. I can hardly stomach it. It smells of Osiris. I can only imagine the dirt he's done wearing it. But if playing his horseman means escaping Philly for good, so be it.

I'm nearly to the corner when I turn back to see Osiris

watching me from his apartment window. He raises his glass as if toasting to my good luck. So far I've been on a losing streak, and I dread the misfortune a toast from Osiris will bring. He's playing me like a pawn. Even if I fail, it wouldn't be the end of him. Men like Osiris always stay two moves ahead. It's how he avoided prison for so long. I'll have to stay sharp. The moment I slip up, he won't waste time asking questions or getting the straight. He'll either feed me to the wolves or bury me himself. And I didn't come this far to let that happen.

I think about the shank I spent months filing down from a toothbrush against the floor of my cell. Back then I contemplated driving the shank into my own gullet. Now, all I yearn to do is drive that shank into the back of Osiris' neck, so he can bleed out surrounded by his goddamn books. But perhaps that's too merciful a death for him? The men he owes probably have better plans for how he ends.

I walk up Passyunk and head north toward Broad. The suit is my new skin, one that seems to diminish my blackness. I've gotten used to white men pulling their girlfriends close when I pass, white women crossing the street a block away when they see me coming. But now that I am in the suit, women's eyes linger. I wonder if I look like a lawyer to them or a therapist on his way home from a hard day of patients—a father with a wife, kids, waiting around a dinner table, placemats set for an early supper?

I pass a white man in a gray pin-stripped business suit carrying a brown leather briefcase. His tie is loosened around his neck and his shirt collar is unbuttoned. His strut is wide, and he's taking up a good portion of the sidewalk. He grins and moves over, allowing me room to pass.

Our eyes meet and he speaks: "How's it going?"

"What? Oh. Fine."

He catches me off-guard and I retort sharply, smiling to clean up my rudeness.

"Has it been one of those days?" he says, pushing back the sweat-dampened hair from his forehead with his palm. "It can't be that bad. I'm sure it'll turn around." He's so engulfed in our one-sided conversation that he nearly bumps into a woman bogged down with groceries. He apologizes to her and chuckles to alleviate his embarrassment.

I can't remember the last time a stranger spoke to me on the streets, or if it's ever happened before. In the South, one could expect a friendly nod or chitchat on the street, but in Philly there's a science to minding your own business. Most people are unloading into cell phones, earphones with music, anything to escape having to deal with folks, having to acknowledge somebody else's existence. You can't control whom you walk past, but you can choose whether or not they exist to you, and for a broke brother like me, I simply wasn't there.

I go into a café, one that is part of a somewhat upscale chain, on the corner of 15th and Locust. The waitress seats me right away and gives me a few minutes to look over the menu. When she returns to my table, I order a turkey sandwich and a coffee with a shot of Kahlua.

The waitress keeps the coffee and Kahlua mix coming, making it a little bit stronger each time. On the third round, she brings me my order. I eat and watch out a window, as people move about the streets—little insects carrying all their briefcases, purses, bags, like crumbs to their nesting grounds.

When I finish my sandwich, the waitress suggests desert—a gourmet fudge brownie with some kind of truffle garnish on top. I decline, and then she takes a seat in the booth and introduces herself as Kim.

"You know, it's cheaper going to a bar if you're looking to drink," she says.

"The caffeine evens things out," I say.

"Don't want to get too loose on your lunch break?"

"That's right."

"What do you do?"

I take another sip of the coffee she's made poison with the sweet liquor. My eyes scan the room. No one seems to notice the brunette girl with deep brown eyes flirting with me, and I question my own insecurity. If she knew I was an ex-convict, she would give me my check early and stay in the back until I paid and left. But to her, I'm a white-collared brother taking the edge off his day.

"I'm a businessman," I say.

She laughs.

"Okay, what kind of business?" she asks.

"I don't like to talk about work."

"Mysterious, are we? Well, I'm a dancer."

"Which club?"

"Ballet," she says, firmly.

"Sorry, I didn't mean to offend you. I've never met a ballet dancer before."

"Well, now you have." Her smile is brilliant and I find myself smiling also.

She reaches over and quickly flicks a piece of lint off my lapel.

"Thanks," I say a bit dryly.

"So you got a name?"

"Paul."

"It's nice to meet you, Paul."

"It's my pleasure, Kim."

"You don't talk much, do you?" she asks.

"I've been accused of being too quiet."

"That means you're a doer. You get things done and don't waste time talking about it. I like that."

"A doer?"

"That's right. Some people are talkers and others are doers. I prefer doers."

My body is still trembling from her touch. I haven't been touched by a woman like that since Tammy.

"I should probably head back to the office," I say.

"Oh, there's an office?" she says. "He finally gives something up."

"We will leave it at that for now."

"That's fine with me. I like a little mystery."

The manager, a hefty man with a three-day shave, calls for Kim. She looks to the clock.

"What an asshole. I still have five minutes left. I get off at six, if you want to make good on a real drink. I know a great bar around the corner."

Before I can answer, she jots her phone number on the napkin and slides out of the booth.

"In case you want a rain check," she says, putting her apron back on. "But hopefully that isn't the case." I watch her slip behind the coffee bar. She's curvy with long well-defined legs and a shapely rear. With every step her heel raises high and her weight is balanced on her toes. She feels my eyes on her and turns around, giving me a seductive leer. I grow warm around my collar, and I'm not sure if it's the Kahlua in the coffee or the beauty behind the bar.

I finish up and pay, tipping her two dollars over what would be considered generous.

Outside the café, I hail a cab.

"Where to?" the cabbie asks, raising his Dutch boy cap an inch above his forehead with his index finger.

"North Philly," I say.

I glance back at the café to see Kim in the window, busing the table for the next customer. She looks up from her task, watching the rear of my cab head down 15th. I had befriended a white woman once who taught English at the prison. She was from Canada originally and when she spoke of it she said that race held no true bearing there, that Canadians had found a way to see past it. The brothers in the class called her a liar, spit on her, exposed themselves to her, and sent her from the classroom defeated, her eyes heavy with tears and the weight of her folly. How could she tell incarcerated men, some facing consecutive life sentences that there was a place outside the prison walls where race didn't matter? Most of the men in the room had blamed their situation specifically on the color of their skin and would go to their graves believing that they were cursed, and being black was the proof. It was thoughts like those that inspired men to wrap bedsheets around their necks and end their stay because no matter what was outside the walls, it would never be seen by the men on the inside and the idea of a paradise on earth was too much to bear.

In prison you were more comforted by the idea of hell than anything else because at least you knew what to expect and had been trained for it. But I gambled on the teacher and convinced myself that a place of racial harmony or at least some equality existed. I envisioned her Canada and it gave me hope. The sheer thought of a place where I could be treated as a man, not as an ex-con, not as a poor black bastard, but just as a man helped keep me sane.

I wonder if like that teacher Kim can't see color. Or am I an experiment? Will she get around her girlfriends after ballet class and say, "Well girls, it's true, black boys are packing." Will she render me an animal? Only calling me when she needs to be satisfied? And will I object to it? Will I tell myself I should be so lucky? And if she did this, how would it be any different from my life with Tammy? How has any woman been different? All of them knew the type of man I was and treated me accordingly. I worked, I drank, and I got high. Tammy wasn't the first. There have been many women who've kept me like a stray cat, but Tammy was the only one I couldn't con—the only one who took me in and gave me a home despite my history. Once I had a girl I wanted to marry, but drinking destroyed it. Sometimes I think about the life I could have had—the life I was supposed to have. And when those hopeless thoughts get the better of me, I let the alcohol consume me until I forget. But lately not even a strong drink has been able to curve the gnawing pain of existence. I have to get out of here. I have to get back to the South. I'm no soothsayer, but I feel a murder coming on. I feel it the way the rain hurts the bones of brothers who have been shot. I've felt it ever since leaving Tammy's brownstone steps, and it's coming on stronger by the day.

Maybe Tammy put a hex on me? Between her sobs, perhaps she muttered words of retribution? Is Karma finally catching up with me? Maybe there's some man, some savage out there lurking and just primed to do me harm. And maybe I deserve it.

I have the cab drop me off at Dougie's apartment. I walk across the street to a laundry mat where I wait, flipping through a magazine about motorcycles and souped-up cars. I survey the building's entrance, watching as people come and go, biding my time until the devilish bastard comes home. I doze off twice, but the sounds of the machines changing cycles prevent me from a deep sleep, and when I awake I see the yellow light in Dougie's window.

I slip into the building after holding the door for a company of kids rambling about spending their allowances at the corner bodega. I head up a flight of stairs, until I get to what if my memory serves correctly is Dougie's door. I remove my suit coat, tie it around my waist and then roll up my shirtsleeves.

I bang on the door so hard the frame rattles. I hear him moving about the apartment, cursing, and as the footsteps get closer to the door, my neck tightens and I grow hot. He unlocks the deadbolt and the door cracks open.

"Paul?" he asks, shocked.

I slam my body into the door and Dougie stumbles back crashing into his coffee table and knocking a lamp to the floor. I grab Dougie by his shirt collar, pull him to my chest and strike him. There isn't much time for Dougie to fight back. He's stunned—lost in that foggy haze when the pain just begins to register in the brain. I deliver two blows to the soft part of his chin, so hard that his teeth plow into his upper lip, leaving it bite-ravaged.

My fist is washed in crimson, and his mouth is starting to swell, the puffy pink meat discernible through the dark of his lips.

"Shit, Paul," he says, spitting blood through his teeth. "Enough,"

I leave Dougie on the couch, holding his mouth, and go into his bathroom. I give myself a good look over in the mirror. Dougie has a light bulb out over the vanity, but I do my best to make sure blood hasn't collected on my borrowed clothes. I hadn't struck anybody in years, and I regret having to have done it to Dougie.

I return to the kitchen and take a cold beer from the fridge. The same cheap brew he gave me the night he perpetrated as my savior.

"Here, put this to the swelling," I say, handing Dougie the beer. He takes it and puts the cold brew to his lips.

I scrounge around Dougie's kitchen looking for a matchbook or a lighter to smoke my last cigarette. I end up lighting it with a rolled up napkin that I stick into the gas burner and then extinguish in the sink before the flame gets too ballsy.

Dougie curses between grunts and moans while I enjoy my smoke.

"Paul, I have good mind to shoot you," he says.

"You don't have the heart for that. Besides, you had it coming. You're lucky. Some fellas wouldn't have stopped there. And to tell you the truth, I had to fight the urge to keep going."

Dougie wipes the blood from his mouth with his shirt.

"I guess you figured I was long dead by now," I say.

"He said he wasn't going to kill you. He just wanted to talk."

"Yeah. Right. Talk. How much did you collect?"

"Ah, man, it's not like that."

"How much?"

"Five hundred."

"Where's the money now?"

"I spent it."

"Where?"

"At the bar with some broad named Tiff."

"You spent it for some bar snatch?"

"Yes."

"Goddamn you, Dougie."

"Shit, man, he said he was just going to ask you some questions. Sorry."

"You're sorry, now. You weren't when you were soiling the sheets."

I grab a kitchen cloth from the counter and toss it to Dougie. He takes the towel and soaks up the fresh blood that's formed in the corner of his mouth.

"Five hundred, huh?"

"I'd give it to you if I had it," he says.

"I don't care about the money. That's over now. You paid with your beating. But in the process I bought something."

"What?"

"Your services. I'm working with Osiris now and you're working for me. You hit the streets. Tell everybody that I'm looking for a man named Franklin Webster and that I'll pay top dollar for whoever can deliver him to me."

"Frank who?"

"Webster! You sent Osiris for me and now you'll put your snitch skills to better use. You tell me where I can find him or next time they'll be fishing you out of the Delaware."

I toss the beer bottle into the trash and walk toward the door.

"You might want to get to a hospital if the swelling doesn't go down," I say, before closing the door behind me. At the end of the hallway is a boy, sitting Indian style, shirtless, wearing flip-flops and shorts cut from a pair of blue jeans, and playing with a toy fire engine.

"Is mister Dougie all right?" he asks.

"He'll be fine. How about you check on him in the morning. Make sure he's feeling better."

"He's sick?"

"Yeah, a cold I think."

"Okay," he says. "I'll check on him."

The boy gives me a highbrow salute and I leave him to his fire engine. The truck's siren echoes through the hallway and slowly fades into silence, as I walk down the stairs and into the lobby. I can't deny that laying hands on Dougie seemed to relieve some stress. I needed to get it out of my system, but the urge to keep pounding was strong. I wanted to bury my fist deep into his skull and it took all the decency in my soul not to. Because in that moment, Dougie was nothing to me—he was less than nothing—and to think how easy it would have been to kill him leaves me feeling ill—just a few moments more and I would have taken another life.

Outside, I feel a few drops of rain as I search for a cab. It's rare for cabs to cruise the neighborhood for fares, so I head north to a donut shop that cabbies frequent for caffeine and sugar fixes preparing for their graveyard shifts. I'm about a block away from the donut shop when the sky cracks open and crystal buckets fall. I run across the street while shielding myself with my suit jacket. By the time I enter the donut shop I'm drenched.

The place is packed with cabbies, some eating, but most looking at me baffled. I fix myself, straightening my suit.

"Any of you cabbies going west?" I ask.

The cabbies look annoyed and one cabbie makes an obscene gesture toward me.

"When we're good and ready!" he shouts, stopping from masticating a jelly-filled donut, the bits and pieces evident on his chin and shirt.

"Have a seat, businessman. Take a load off." A cabbie wearing a hooded sweatshirt and a black baseball cap pulls a chair out from the table. He's Middle Eastern with an accent still native to his home country. I have a seat next to him.

"I'll take you as soon as I'm done with my coffee," he says. "You're not in any rush are you?"

"No, as long as I'm out of the rain," I say.

"Yeah, it's really coming down. Philly always gets a ton of rain at the end of summer. It's how you know we're going to have a wet fall."

Two cops enter the donut shop. They scan the room and then walk toward the counter to order.

"You coming from work?" the cabbie asks.

"Yeah, a late meeting."

"What do you do?"

"I'm a salesman."

"That right? What do you sell?"

"Wholesale electronics . . . to businesses mostly, like PDAs, organizers, personal GPS, things like that."

I flash the GPS device Osiris slipped me to help convince him.

"How's that working out for you?"

"Business is good. It could always be better though. With the economy like it is, you have to grateful for every cent."

"You look like a solid salesman," he says. "There's a good confidence about you."

"Thanks."

He takes another sip from his cup and his eyes shift to the two cops who are now sitting behind me.

"Got something on your shirt," he says in a low voice.

I look down to see a few diluted blotches of blood, Dougie's blood.

"Did somebody try for a refund?" He follows the question with an awkward chuckle. I'm speechless; I give him a pleading look.

"Don't worry, my friend," he says. "You head out first and I'll follow. The cops won't be the wiser."

I get up and start moving toward the exit. The cabbie waits a few seconds, tosses his cup and heads out behind me.

The rain is beginning to subside and the parking lot is slick, black, and a vapor-like mist lingers just above the street.

"Cab is over here," he says, pointing to a white cab with a red-checkered pattern along the side and a dent in the driver's side door.

The interior of the cab is brown vinyl and it smells of wet

dog. He adjusts his mirror, so he can get a good look at my face.

"Thanks," I say.

"Don't mention it," he says. "You don't really sell electronics, do you?"

"No."

"I figured as much."

"Maybe it's best we don't talk about it."

"Sorry, I get nosy. Too curious for my own good says the wife. Where we headed?"

"The Royale on Walnut."

I figure checking into the Royale is as safe as any other cheap lodging. I'll use the nosy manager as a lookout. He'll keep me abreast on things and hopefully any potential troubles at bay.

"Okay," he says, as he shifts into reverse.

We sit at a stoplight and the rain starts up again. My eyes track the drops as they land on the window, stream down the glass, consuming other drops in their path like cancer cells, and then disappear down the side of the cab. He tunes the radio to the local public news station. The jockey's voice is machine-like, a programmed drone spewing his political jargon onto the airways. I take out the book I borrowed from Osiris and flip to the first page.

I begin to read.

"What you reading?" asks the cabbie.

I hold up the book. Written in white on the cover is *The Science of Man: The Journal of David Hume.*

"I've never heard of it. What is it about?"

"Philosophies on life, justice, society, God, stuff like that. His thoughts poured out onto paper."

"Sounds like pretty heavy stuff. What are his thoughts on justice?"

"You really want to know?"

"Sure. I'm always interested in peoples takes on things. I may not look like it, driving this cab and all, but I'm a thinker and a reader."

"Hume says if this world was truly just, then there would be no need for justice. If we all had enough, if nature had provided a way for us to live without the burden of labor, there would be no poor, no anguish—no crime. But even if we didn't have enough food, enough resources, if man truly had a generous heart, then we would care for each other. Crime is a result of the split between those who have and those who don't."

"Sounds like he's saying man is the problem?"

"Maybe, or maybe it's just too much responsibility, too much burden for man alone. So we need religion, something to turn to."

"Like God?"

"Yeah, like God. I guess."

"That's heavy, man, but interesting. You say his name is Hume?"

"David Hume."

"I might have to look into his stuff. Is this good, buddy?" He pulls in front of the Royale and shifts into park.

"Yes." I take out the seven bucks I owe him, tipping him two singles.

"You take care," he says. I shut the door and the cabbie continues on his route.

The lobby is quiet as I walk toward the marble counter. The manager is busy on the computer and doesn't notice me right away. He looks up from the screen and sees my suit before my face.

"Sir, how may I help—?"

His head slowly rises until our eyes meet.

"Checking back in, are we?"

"Yes," I say. "Room 207."

I request room 207 again because of the location. I can see Walnut and I'll have a good view of folks before they enter the hotel.

"It looks like room 207 is still available," he says. "Paying with cash?"

"Yes."

"Forty-five dollars," he says.

I pay him.

The manager plucks away at the computer and prints a form. I sign it and he hands me my room key.

"Is that it?" I ask.

"Yes, that's it. Enjoy your stay."

"Whatever."

I walk toward the elevator.

"It's still not working, sir," the manager says rather hastily.

I take the stairs and tell myself the exercise won't hurt.

The hotel is even quieter than I remember. The construction work and broken elevator must still be keeping folks away.

I enter 207 and turn on the entry light to see my way. I remove the book from my pocket and set it on the desk. I take off my shirt, run some cold water in the bathroom sink, and soak it until the clear water gradually becomes red. I have a seat on the edge of the bed and remember Marcus. I can still smell his cigarette in the duvet, and I realize they haven't cleaned the room since my last departure. I think about calling down to the front desk and demanding a clean set of linen, but the familiar scent is comforting. Marcus' spirit, has he returned? Has he come to exact his revenge on me? Or perhaps direct me to his killer? I listen for a name, for a whisper, for something ethereal. But there is nothing, just the whistle of my breathing, the tap of the rain, and I know even Marcus has forsaken me.

I dial Tammy, wanting to hear her voice. I know I should leave her be, but the way things ended isn't sitting well.

"Hello?" she answers.

"Tammy," I say.

There's silence.

"Tammy, I want to talk."

Then dial tone.

I slam the phone down on the base and rest my head back on the pillow, focusing on the tatty stucco ceiling. Tammy's face forms from the pallid bumps of the stucco and then slowly morphs into Kim's—first her nose, then her eyes and finally her lips. I stare at the image for a moment, and the thought of Kim stimulates me from my chest to my groin. Is she the drug I need, a remedy that will help me forget? If only for a few hours can I escape the thoughts of Marcus, Tammy, and Osiris?

I dial Kim and she answers.

"Hello?"

"Kim?"

"Yes."

"It's Paul, from the café."

"Funny time to be calling," she says, chuckling uneasily.

"I'm sorry. I have a horrible sleeping schedule and sometimes I forget the rest of the world doesn't share my clock. It was my mistake. I'll let you go."

"Wait. It's fine. I was just reading a magazine. Is everything okay?"

"I've had better."

"I take it that the coffee shots this afternoon were evidence of that."

"Yes and there's more to come. I'm going to stop in at the liquor store before it closes. Do you prefer red or white?"

"Is that supposed to be an invitation?" she asks, somewhat taken aback.

"Only if you say yes. If it's a no, then it was a harmless attempt to get to know you better that didn't go over very well."

Kim laughs and then follows with a sigh.

"When I suggested a drink I was thinking more of a bar."

"You're right. That was a little forward of me, sorry. Maybe another time then."

"Well, maybe one drink," she says readily.

"I'll be a perfect gentleman."

"Oh, I'm not worried. I knew when I met you that you had a way about you—something gentle, sweet."

Tammy's words coming out of Kim's mouth.

"Paul?" she says. "You still there?"

"Ah, yes. Sorry."

"You wandered off there."

"It's a bad line."

"Good. I thought I was boring you. Where do you stay?"

"The Royale Hotel. Room 207."

"A hotel?"

"I'm between living situations."

"I see. All right, give me thirty and make it red."

"Red it is."

I rush into the liquor store and then into the 24-hour quick mart to pick up a few toiletries and chewing gum. I make it back to the hotel with enough time to brush my teeth and wash up before Kim shows.

We polish off the bottle of wine and Kim begins to tell me about her travels and the places she's visited when she danced on tour: Morocco, London, China, Guam, South Africa, and Dubai.

"The dance company pays for everything?" I ask.

She giggles, slowly placing her glass on the table—the red residue on her lips.

"Yes. It's all part of the deal."

"Sounds like a great deal. I wish I had rhythm."

She giggles, "Please. I bet you can dance."

"I'm afraid that's a bet you'd lose. The last time I danced I rolled my ankle. I was in bed for two days."

"Ah, poor baby," she says caressing my hand. "Do you travel much?"

"Not as much as I'd like and mostly in the states," I say.

"It's a beautiful world, Paul. Sometimes it blows my mind. One day you just have to see the sunrise over the Serengeti. Seeing it is like . . ." She searches for the words. "It's like being reborn."

"Reborn?"

"Yes, like the world is starting over every morning and anything is possible—like yesterday was just a memory."

She speaks with passion. I get lost in her deep dark eyes until I see my reflection in them and break away from my stare.

"Have you always wanted to dance?" I ask.

"Yes, since I can remember. My mother started me in classes when I was very young. Are you close with your parents?"

"No. My mother is dead and my father left when I was a kid."

"Oh, I'm sorry."

"I was too little to remember. My grandfather cared for me."

"So you have *someone*?" she asks.

"Had," I say, emphasizing the past tense.

"Oh," she says. I can tell the conversation is putting a damper on the mood, but I don't want to be too abrupt.

"He passed away recently, but he lived a great full life," I say, leaving it at that.

"That's all we can hope for I guess."

The rain begins to pick up again and I move toward the window, gazing at the full moon washed gray with storm clouds. I press my palm to the glass. The glass is cooler than I expect, and then I remember the air is cooler higher up. Kim approaches from behind and rests her head on my shoulder. She kisses me, just brushing her lips against the tiny hairs of my neck. She presses her chest against my back and I can feel her heartbeat. She smells of a fragrance that I'm not familiar with, something expensive, maybe European? I take a deep whiff of her bosom and the rotten scent of Marcus fades.

I take her by the waist, squeezing her breast and placing my palm on her cheek. She doesn't feel like Tammy. Her skin is colder and doesn't feel as thick, like she would be more susceptible to bruising.

I kiss her hard, sealing my lips with hers until we both violently gasp for air. She tastes like Merlot. I dip my hand into the crotch of her jeans, breaching the security of her button fly. Her pants fall to the floor. I carry her to the bed, and she begins to remove my undershirt. I free her breasts from her blouse and then completely from her bra. She wets her lips with the tip of her tongue and then unbuttons my pants. I slide her panties down past her knees, where they dangle from her left foot, until she shakes them to the floor.

Her nipples are like small pencil erasers, and I'm startled by the drastic contrast of her skin against mine. She glows against me, my bare chest catching the shine of the moonlight and my brown skin merging into hers—an amalgamation of flesh.

I'm so used to Tammy—the placement of her moles, the width of her birthmark and the way her left breast hangs slightly lower than her right. It's as if I've been programmed with the schematics of her body and logistics of our sex. I automatically touch Kim where Tammy would like, expecting the same reaction, but receiving nothing. I explore the small cluster of freckles on the back of her neck, the tiny indention in her left shoulder and the rough patch of skin above her right knee. There's no territory that is uncharted and gradually our sex becomes something unfamiliar, an act that I can feel. Something I almost forgot existed, a sex with emotion—like making love.

The cell phone rings and she begs me not to stop, but I do, knowing what's at stake if I don't answer.

"Hello?"

It's Osiris on the other end calling for an update.

"How are things?" he asks.

"Things are fine," I say.

"Really? You don't sound fine. You sound out of breath."

"Just ran up the stairs. Damn elevator is broken here at the hotel."

"Well, that's not good. The Royale right?"

"I see that GPS is coming in handy."

Kim massages my neck, delivering small kisses to my back and then down my arm.

"Look, I better get some sleep," I say. "Big day tomorrow."

"That's what I like to hear. I'll check in with you tomorrow." He speaks with more arrogance than I can stand.

"Yeah. Sure."

I hang up the phone.

"Your wife?" Kim asks with suspicion.

"No. My boss."

"Your boss calls you at this hour?"

"I'm kind of under the gun."

Kim's kisses come to a halt around my elbow.

"Will it always be like this?" she asks.

"Like what?" I ask, dropping my shoulder so her hand falls to the bed.

"All the mystery and everything being so hush, hush. Will you ever let me in?"

"Is that what you want? To be let in?"

Her eyes are hopelessly glossy. "I'd like this to be more if that's possible."

"Kim, things are complicated."

"So that's a no?"

"I just don't know what to tell you. My work requires—"

"Secrecy."

"Discretion," I say, correcting her.

She runs her index finger across my shoulder, examining an old stab wound I suffered in prison.

"I like you, Paul. I really do. The fact this happened tonight is not the norm for me."

"Not the norm?" I say. "What is the norm?"

"I just don't go to bed with men I've only known a few hours," she says, defensive.

If only Kim knew the truth. Part of me is angry at her for being suckered so easily. I'm the wolf her mother probably warned her about, the wolf all girls are warned about— cunning, dangerous. It's girls like her that end up on the six o'clock news after being found in some alley, sliced to rivets, and bleeding from where life grows. What if I had killed a man for the suit and booked a night in a hotel before disappearing for good? She doesn't know me from Adam. I've spent nights locked in cells with men who wouldn't hesitate to rip the life right out of her. Men who told me of their accomplishments, who gloated and became visibly aroused, stroking their cocks under bedsheets while reminiscing about the things they did to women. And not just women, but girls, young girls a few years shy of Kim, girls who never saw the threat, who never saw the beast looming.

Kim, you fool.

I get out of bed and put my shirt back on, along with my pants.

"Paul, are you all right?" she asks.

"You shouldn't be here. I think you should go."

"Was it something I said?"

"No. I'll call you a cab."

"Okay," she says with a quiver. "If that's what you want."

She gets out of bed and puts her clothes back on. Not bothering to put on her bra, she opts to stuff it into her purse. She fixes her hair, teasing her bangs and brushing the loose strands behind her ears with her fingers.

I move toward the window, gazing outward with my back toward her. She takes a few steps toward the door and then pauses, facing me and hoping for a punch line or at least an apology, but I don't oblige her. I simply stare out the window, counting the seconds until she's gone.

"Will you call?" she asks.

I dig into my pocket and take out a few bills. I walk over to her, offering them. Kim looks at the money, keeping her hands tight on the strap of her purse.

"I said it wasn't necessary." Her voice is stern now and her glare severe. She's insulted, and I know the gesture has made her feel cheap.

"I can walk you down and have the manager dial for a cab," I say.

"It's a busy street. I can hail one."

Kim leaves the room, slowly pulling the door closed behind her. I want to chase after her and explain that it's not her, that it's me. But every excuse that comes to mind feels like I'd just be turning the knife clockwise so the wound won't close. I had assumed Kim wouldn't care, that she was looking for a night of cheap sex and that she would go on about her business never questioning the outcome. But I was wrong. Kim was looking for something, and for whatever reason she thought she saw it in me. I had made her genuinely happy. If only for a short while we both forgot about our troubles. I recognized the look in her eyes. Tammy had looked at me the same way once. Kim was content, maybe even taken with me. The thought of a future, our future became overwhelmingly real to her, and in a matter of minutes I shattered it. Whatever Kim felt for me, I wanted it to die. Not just for her sake, but also for mine. If I'm to survive, I can't have thoughts of Kim racing in my head, weak thoughts. I have to stay sharp, alert, and hungry. Not a glimmer of happiness. There can be no hope. Not until Osiris is satisfied and I'm on my bus counting the hours until Philly is a memory. Only then can I put an end to this nightmare.

I look out the window toward the street watching as Kim attempts to hail a cab. She shields herself from the rain with a newspaper. There's a slight gust and her hair tosses in the wind escaping from behind her ears. Even from three stories up I can't deny her beauty, and as hard as it is to watch her, I can't turn away. A cab pulls up and before disappearing into the backseat she looks up at my window. She wipes the water from her eyes and then gets into the cab, and I wish to never see her again.

Morning comes. I get showered and walk down Walnut to the Brooks Brothers store. The salesman looks at me. He's panicky, but composed. I probably look like a homeless man to him, or maybe a thief looking to jack his register. He surveys my clothes: a tired undershirt, a wrinkled suit coat, and pants with a cell phone bulge in the right pocket. The book tucked in my waistband.

"Sir, are you looking for something off the rack or do you need to be fitted?" he asks, managing his unease.

"Dress shirts?"

"This way, please."

He's a slim man with an auburn moustache and small frameless glasses. His hands are riddled with age spots and his skin is tight and dry, with a red tinge of rosacea. It's something I recognize from Tammy's medical book. He directs me toward stacks of dress shirts in a variety of colors.

"I'll need black," I say.

"Is this for a specific occasion?" he asks.

"No."

"If you're looking for versatility, black is the way to go. It's something you can wear to a business meeting or even a funeral." He smiles, amused by his rather morbid joke.

He removes a solid black silk shirt and holds it up for me to inspect. I run my hands over the fabric and check the price. It's a bit more than I'm prepared to spend. Then I remember I need boxer shorts and undershirts. He directs me to the underwear section. I grab the cheapest packs and do the quick math in my head. The shirt, underwear, plus tax will leave me with thirty dollars and some change. I've made due with less.

I have him ring up the sale.

Fifteen minutes later, I walk out wearing the shirt, along with the packages of underwear. I return to the hotel, drop off my purchases and then hail a cab to Dougie's apartment. Considering it's the weekend, I imagine Dougie to be sitting on the couch, watching football highlight tapes and guzzling beer. When I arrive at his apartment building, I wait five minutes before the door swings open and an elderly tenant walks out pulling a basket stroller. I gain entry and make my way upstairs to Dougie's door. The television is blaring, and

I deliver two heavy pounds until the door lock unlatches.

"Look, I told you . . . ," he says, pausing before the door swings open to reveal him irritated and sweaty in a pair of boxer shorts and a tank top. His dreadlocks are knotted and kinky. The cheap beer in his hand is foaming at the mouth.

"I'd have the rent tom—" Dougie nearly drops his beer when he sees me.

He makes a run toward his bedroom. He's about six steps in before I snatch him back, pulling the two straps of his tank top and retracting them like bungee cord. He tightens up his shoulders and then takes a swing at me, missing me completely and succumbing to a violent coughing fit.

"You're out of shape, Dougie."

"What the hell you want now?" he asks, gasping for breath.

"I just want to talk," I say.

"Man, I don't know anything."

I kick the door shut and make sure I don't take my eyes off of Dougie. Even though his body is riddled with old football injuries, he's still strong and could lay me out cold with the right punch.

"Come on, Paul. My lip is just starting to feel better."

Dougie's split lip has closed, but there's a deep crease of a scar and a speckled blood blister that looks like it's about to burst at any minute.

"I didn't come to fight. Just tell me what you know about Franklin Webster and I'll be on my way."

Dougie plops down on the couch.

"Franklin? He's a cat from Dorchester. From what I can gather he's an average dealer."

"What else?"

"He's a white boy, supposed be smart. They call him Whiz. What's all this matter to you anyway?"

"I have to collect a debt from him. One of Osiris," I say.

"Osiris has you collecting debts for him?"

"It's a business arrangement, so I can get the hell out of here."

"You trust him?"

"I don't have much of a choice. Besides, trust will get you killed in this city. You taught me that."

"Come off that. I made a mistake. I'm still your man."

"Yeah, right, we're aces," I say. "So where exactly can I find Frank?"

"I don't have an address. But I heard he might be living off Baltimore. Nobody seems to know for sure or they ain't telling. I know what he drives, though. Maybe it'll help you out. It's a red vintage Mustang with Massachusetts plates."

"How do you know this?"

"Creeping around the precinct you hear things. He's pushing dope on the Ivy Leaguers in University City. The cops have had trouble getting hard evidence on him. As soon as they get close to making an arrest they get the bureaucratic block. My guess is someone is protecting him, someone with juice."

"I don't give a damn about that," I say. "As long as he pays."

"You be careful. It's not our territory. Cops play for keeps up there."

"The beast plays for keeps everywhere, Dougie."

"Look, I don't want beef between us, Paul. I even turned your paperwork in. You're a free man. No more parole."

"And I'm supposed to be grateful to you?"

"Now you can take your little trip. I made that happen for you."

"It's what you should have done in the first place."

"Man, get off my back! You ain't no better than me. You're just like me—a nobody. You're just another broke-ass, Philly ex-con. You'll die in these streets, just like all them others. "

"That's where you're wrong. I'm not going to let this city kill me. Football was your way out. You could have become a coach—college, high school, a damn peewee league—maybe even talking sports on the news. People loved you. But now look at you. You're a goddamn parole officer, not even a cop—a lackey, a babysitter for boys pretending to be men. And in the end, you're no better than the animals you're paid to watch."

Dougie rises from the couch and lunges at me. I quickly push him back down with a blow to his chest, and he cowers. This time I leave Dougie intact, but not his pride.

Outside, I walk a block to the bus stop and wait about twenty minutes, flipping through my book and people-watching. When the Septa bus arrives, I board and head west toward University City, an affluent part of Philadelphia. I once took Tammy to an Asian fusion restaurant there. We received poor service, but great food.

I have the bus drop me off at 30th and Pine. The streets are animated with bicyclists, mothers pushing strollers, college students wielding baseball bats and bouncing basketballs, out-of-work artists peddling their watercolors and acrylics. I buy a falafel sandwich from a street vendor and head toward Baltimore Avenue, admiring the Victorian homes and how clean the streets are kept compared to Dougie's neighborhood. You can always tell the wealthier parts of the city based on how well the streets are kept.

I walk up and down Baltimore, scanning for the red Mustang. I stroll onto the lawn of what I gather from the loud rock music is a house filled with college students. I think I see the tail end of the sports car parked in the driveway, but as I get closer a yelping mutt darts from around the house and rears its teeth. I back away, but not before getting a better look at the car's license plate. It's a Pennsylvania plate, the yellow, blue, and white aluminum, a symbol of the impossible nature of my task.

Feeling a bit discouraged and foolish, I take a seat across the street at the Septa Rail Station and read two more chapters of David Hume. I take breaks to watch the cars pass on the off-chance that I'll catch a view of the Mustang. I watch college kids come in and out of the Victorian rentals, while trying to imagine what Frank looks like. Is he tall, short, husky? Does he look like a frat boy? Is that his cover, a way to duck the cops if they're looking for him? I read through chapter four before dozing off on the bench with the book open on my lap.

When I awake, the sun is already beginning to set, dispersing an earthy orange over the horizon. My mouth is dry and I desperately need a smoke. I feel the heavy gaze of a passerby and get up to stretch my legs. I can't help but marvel at the fact I've slept this long without being bothered by the police.

I give the block one last walk. This time I walk Baltimore until I get to 47th and leave University City for West Philadelphia. I turn back when the street lamps get scarce and the thick aroma of marijuana permeates the air. I pass a group of fellas bumping rap music from a car stereo. They're passing a clear liquor bottle around in a semicircle. They pause a moment, snickering and watching me. It's the type of attention I don't need. To a stick-up kid I look like an easy mark—a lost businessman, on foot no less, caught after dark in a neighborhood he has no business being in. Considering my growing irritability and the fact it's the longest I've gone without a cigarette, I know turning back before trouble sets in is the right decision.

I chew a stick of gum to soothe my ache for a smoke and

walk back down Baltimore. In a matter of blocks the homes go from lower class to upper-middle. It's never been so clear to me until now. Life in Philly is a matter of blocks. You go a few blocks west and your neighbor may be a dope dealer, you go east, toward Penn and your neighbor is a professor of math and science. Two different worlds, five blocks apart and somehow they are co-existing. But what world is Franklin living in? Dougie's so-called lead left me sitting on a bench all day looking for a phantom Mustang.

I'm still tired and some sleep could do me good. Returning late-night and searching the party scene for Frank may prove more fruitful.

I walk to the 174 bus stop and hope the bus is running on the fifteen-minute schedule. I wait for about ten minutes before the bus marked for Center City swings its door open and a thick dark-skinned sister pesters me to hurry up and get on.

"Come on. Any day now, honey." She smacks gum and taps her left foot to signify the pace I should be moving. I get on the bus, dropping a handful of change into the fare deposit. I search for a seat, ignoring my transfer ticket, which pops out of the machine. The bus is packed and the passengers all measure me up. The black folks first look at my suit, some giving a cynical "uh huh" glare and rolling their eyes, as if it to say *Who's this brother think he is? Like his shit don't stink.*

I approach an open seat next to a young Latina with a flawless russet complexion and large door-knocker earrings with the word *Flossy* crafted into them. She quickly places her book bag on the seat, preventing me from sitting next to her. A white woman notices and offers me a seat, removing her purse and giving me a friendly nod.

"It's fine," I say. "I'll stand. Thanks."

I hold onto the handrail as the bus pulls away from the stop and creeps to a red light.

If it weren't for the loud banging and crackle of the muffler on the Mustang, I wouldn't have noticed the red blur that entered the intersection as quickly as it came out and then sped up Baltimore, turning a hard right into an alleyway. A 1968 red muscle car, a cherry and nearly stock, except for the shotgun muffler and 24-inch chrome rims—proof that its owner is not a collector or an appreciator.

I rush to the front of the bus.

"I need to get off," I say.

"What?" the driver asks.

"Open the door, please. I gotta get off."

"Ain't no refund," she says, bug-eyed, gum wedged in her clinched jaw.

"That's fine. Just let me off, damn it!"

She swings the door open and I jump the step that reads CAUTION in large white letters, landing on the concrete and nearly toppling over. I race up Baltimore—my shin splints producing a throbbing pain, and by the time I reach the alley I'm out of breath, coughing up yellow and regretting the day I picked up a cigarette. The alley leads to a narrow street, cobblestone with well-kept row houses. Each door is individualized with designer doorknockers, windows, and brass numbering. The Mustang exhaust is still fresh in the air—the smell of burnt oil and high-octane gas. I hear a door slam at the end of the street and move toward it. The road dead-ends at three garages, each secured with locks. I stand for a moment analyzing the locks: one lock is caked outside with rust and the keyhole is sealed with grime and debris, the other lock is a padlock and something a college student would use to protect mommy and daddy's eco-friendly compact, and the last lock is a thick titanium master reinforced with copper. I'm positive that inside is the red Mustang—the hood still warm.

Unlike the lock, nothing about the houses seems to say Franklin Webster, and I have no other option but to wait. I sit on a low brick wall that lines the cobblestone road. The silence is sickening. I'm desperate for a sign of life, for the heavy bass of a boom box, a loud television, anything to remind me that the trail hasn't gone cold, that I truly saw the Mustang and that Frank is near.

I notice a plaque mounted on a street lamp that tells the history of the cobblestone road: "1752, this road was the site of Benjamin Franklin's kite experiments . . ." And today it's the site of Paul Little's failure.

The streets are crowded with college students—groups of kids sporting UPENN shirts and baseball caps heading into the local coffee shops and pizza parlors. I've never set foot on a college campus or been around students. It's another world, one of wealth and privilege. I should envy them. I should be thinking about all the wasted opportunities in my life—the chances I've had to make something of myself, but didn't. I was simply dealt a different hand, and a man can't cry over his hand. He either has to play it or fold. And as easy as it is to blame my circumstances for what I've become, I don't.

I walk across the street to the coffee shop, looking over my shoulder in case Franklin Webster makes an appearance. The shop is filled with locals and students. I look at the menu board and the prices are evidence that it's not a chain; everything is priced three dollars more than the chain shops that are scattered all over the city.

There are a few customers in front of me in line and all seem to know what they want. The line moves quickly and when I reach the counter, I order a black coffee and a rosemary scone.

"These are just divine," the barista says, as she removes the scone from the glass case and places it in a bag. She hands me my coffee and judging by the color and the stiff aroma I'll be up till morning.

"Thanks," I say.

"You're welcome!" she says too bubbly. I wonder if her chipper attitude is real or enforced by the managers.

I take a few napkins from the kiosk and head out. I'm nearly to the door when an older man with silver hair and a brown wrinkled leathery complexion taps me on the shoulder.

"I prefer Martin Buber," he says.

"What?"

"I haven't read this in years," he says, taking the book from my hand. "Is this a first edition?"

"I don't know," I say, perturbed. The audacity of him to snatch the book from my hand without asking has bad thoughts running through my head, all involving the piping hot coffee splashing his polo shirt and scalding his face. I can make it look like an accident. The lid on my coffee cup isn't on tight, and I'm prone to trip. . . .

He flips through the book and then sticks out his hand for a more formal introduction.

"Professor Gerald Smith, I teach English at the university. Are you a student?"

"No," I say.

"Wait. Let me guess, you're the new guy they hired over in the Philosophy Department?"

The man is speaking so loud that the whole coffee shop is beginning to look. He's too close to me. The sacred feet of personal space obviously don't exist in his book, and every time he opens his mouth I get spit on. I take a few steps back, cocking my head and glaring, as if to say: "Give me my book back, you annoying son-of-a-bitch." But he doesn't get the hint. He continues to ramble and then pulls out a chair from a circular table.

"Sit with me," he says. "I'd really love to pick your brain."

I take a look at the table: books, a crossword puzzle, term papers, a cell phone, and a pack of mint chewing gum. All the things a man needs to fight boredom. It's as if he's been waiting for this moment, for me to walk into this coffee shop just so he can "pick my brain".

"I really should be going," I say in my best professorial voice.

"I'm sure it can wait. Please?"

I can feel the eyes of the customers watching us. I turn around to see a woman paused over an open book, her nose turned up, her head resting on her fist. She sighs and then rolls her eyes at me.

I give in and take a seat.

"So, tell me how do you like Penn so far?" he says. "It's a bit of a mad house with a week left before the students leave. It's a lot to take in and I'm sure there's a lot of schmoozing, meeting people. The president putting you on display, but come fall your novelty will wear off."

"It's fine."

I can tell he's one of those educated blacks who are more comfortable being the odd man in a sea of white intellectuals and rich kids. At a black college, they would probably question his blackness and his dedication to the struggle. Here he's special, like the talking horse that used to come on television when I was a kid, smart, but a beast of burden nonetheless. I'm sure it's how the other professors would describe him. Old Gerald Smith keeps on task and would never rock the boat, probably holding out for an office with a window and an invitation to the president's Labor Day picnic. Or maybe I'm being too harsh? Perhaps Gerald just reminds me of the black teachers I had in elementary school, the one's who would tell me to ignore it or just shake it off after I got called a coon in the lunch room. Being one of only three blacks in school, it was an everyday occurrence.

"You know what books you're going to teach next semester?" he asks.

He doesn't wait for me to answer. Not that I have an answer.

"You're a lot younger than I thought you would be," he says.

"I get that a lot."

"I guess you love all that existential hoopla. It's entertaining. Not very practical, but entertaining."

I smile in agreement. Believing if I speak it will only encourage him.

"I would love for you to join our faculty reading group," he says. "I'm the president and the founder. We meet once a week. It would be nice to have a new face. I'm sure you could bring a different perspective to the group. Something we all could benefit from."

He shoves a gourmet cookie into his mouth and then swallows it down with his coffee.

My cell phone rings and I quickly pull it from my suit coat. It's Osiris, and though normally the ring would provoke bile to kick up in my belly, this time I'm relieved.

"Excuse me," I say. "I have to take this." I quickly remove myself from the table and high-tail it out of the coffee shop.

"Yeah?"

"You get my money?" Osiris asks.

"I'm working on it," I say. "It would have helped if you had given me an address."

"Shit, Frank ain't hard to find. You find the coke and you find Frank Webster. Look, things are getting hot. Moiye was camped out in front of my apartment all night and into the morning."

"You invite him in for breakfast?" I ask.

"I like a man who can still find humor in the grimmest of circumstances. But I'm not one of those men."

"My grandfather always said sometimes you have to laugh to keep from crying."

"Sure. It's always funny until someone gets hurt or ends up in jail. Moiye is building his case. So be aware, he may know you're in the mix."

"I haven't seen him. I've been on the move all day. Buses and cabs. . . ."

"Good," he says. "In case he leans on you, hems you up, you best not tell him anything. Not a word. Or we'll have problems. I still have eyes and ears out there."

"Are we done?"

"Yes, until tomorrow. . . ."

I hang up and look back toward the coffee shop to see Gerald Smith pestering another patron.

I walk back toward the cobblestone road with the hope that Franklin will make himself known. As I get closer, I see a group of boys lugging a beer keg into an open door of a row house. There's loud music coming from the house and the flicker of a strobe light from upstairs. Groups of students drinking beer have congregated out front, some with for-ty-ounce bottles wrapped in brown paper bags and 16-ounce silver bullets. I pass a group of skinny brunettes and blondes in cut-off shorts and halter-tops chattering as they approach the door.

"Frank better be here," one of the girls says as she straight-ens her ponytail and then adjusts the string of her thong so that it's visibly rising from her shorts.

"That shit we scored last time wasn't bad," another girl says, while digging in her purse and removing lip gloss and then applying it to her lips.

I relax some, now that I know Franklin is inside. I watch as the girls haggle at the door with a beefy boy wearing a cap backward. I drink my coffee and finish my scone. I keep out of the streetlight so I'm not easily noticed. When I am noticed, I look toward the other brownstones and pace as if I'm lost and searching for an address.

I let the party thicken before slowly moving toward the front door. A girl comes rushing out, followed by a dark-haired boy in a blue-striped polo shirt. She brushes past me with her hands over her mouth and then releases her stomach contents into a bush, while the dark-haired boy holds her hair back.

"Shit, Mel," the boy says. "Maybe you better stick to beer tonight." He laughs wildly and deviously runs his hand over her breasts. The girl is either willing to endure the grope or too drunk to object—maybe even a bit of both. I plant my right boot on the first step and wait until the beefy boy turns around to question me. He's so distracted with the blonde that he hardly notices me, but when he does, he straightens up and crosses his arms, puffing out his chest while sizing me up.

"Who are you?" he asks.

"Paul. I'm here for Franklin."

"Frank? He invited you?"

"That's right. We have business."

The boy leans closer to me and drops his hands to his sides.

"You a cop?" he asks in a low voice.

"Nope."

"You have to tell me if you are, or it's entrapment. I'm pre-law. So don't try to bullshit."

"I'm not a cop, kid."

"Hold on," he says as he removes a cell phone from his pocket. His hand shakes some and he's sweaty around his neck and underarms. He's too young for the shakes and his dilated pupils tell me he's on something, something strong.

He dials and presses the phone to his ear. He ends the call after a few seconds.

"He's not answering," the boy mumbles.

"I'm just here to talk. I told him I'd be by tonight. We have some business that really shouldn't wait and I don't have time to waste with you when I can be inside rapping with him."

He's apprehensive, looking over my head and searching the darkness for cops or whoever he thinks may be hiding there.

"I don't want any trouble in here," he says, as he flashes me a switchblade from his pants cargo pocket.

"Just here to talk," I say, reassuringly. "No trouble."

"Okay, he's upstairs," he says.

He moves aside and I walk into the house.

Inside, I'm greeted by the dank smell of marijuana and a deep tanned brunette in wedged sandals. Her skin is the color of peanut butter, and I can't help but stare at her. I wonder if she's black-Irish or Sicilian? Maybe she's a sister passing as a white girl? Or maybe I'm just desperate to see another brown face?

"Take a picture," she says, taking a sip of beer from a long neck, "it'll last longer,"

"What?"

"I'm only kidding," she says.

"Oh. I didn't mean anything by it."

"No. I'm flattered. What's with the suit? Are you a T.A. or

something? You know they fire teaching assistants for party-ing with students."

"I'm not a T.A. I'm looking for someone."

"Guy or girl?"

"Franklin Webster."

She laughs, holding the beer neck between two fingers.

"Oh my God, his last name is Webster?" she says. "That's great."

"You know where he is? He seems to be a hard man to find."

"Frank is not hard to find. He's upstairs. I'll take you to him."

"All right."

"But first you have to promise me something," she says grinning.

"Promise you something? Like what?"

"Not to leave here before dancing with me," she says, fol-lowed by a smile that's more innocent than seductive.

I look to the living room where people are dancing, grinding—dry humping each other to music with so much bass that the pictures rattle against the walls.

"Okay." I agree, hoping she'll hurry up and take me to Frank.

"I'm Devon," she says.

"Paul."

The exchange doesn't deserve a handshake. It's neither formal nor casual and hopefully she'll forget about me after another round.

"You want something to drink, a beer or something?" she asks.

"What?" I say. "I can't hear over this music."

"A beer, you know? Something to drink?"

"No. No, thanks."

She turns on her heel and heads upstairs, switching her hips back and forth with me in tow. We maneuver past people on the stairs, some conversing, some kissing, and others trying to make their way down to the dance floor. We arrive at a closed door; red light can be seen under it.

"He's in here," she says. "Try not to let him bore you to death." She kisses me on the cheek and disappears into the crowd of people posted on the steps. I turn the knob and slowly open the door. Red party bulbs light the room. The jazz that is playing is in stark contrast to the rap and R&B downstairs, and I figure if Frank likes jazz he has to be somewhat reasonable.

A girl appears from a back room and takes a seat on a tan leather sofa next to a fair-haired white boy wearing a political button on the lapel of his sport shirt and a skinny red-and-black plaid tie. None of his clothes match, and he either gets dressed in the dark or he's color-blind. He removes a small vile of coke from his pocket and then sprinkles a bit of the substance on the table. He rolls up a bill and then snorts the coke. He doesn't finish the line and leaves the rest for the girl. She snorts the line, sniffs, and then licks her finger collecting the residue of coke and rubbing it against her gums. I recognize the girl from earlier by the thong that's now settled high on her hips.

"Frank, let's go downstairs and dance," the girl says, tugging at his tie.

"You know me better than that. That music they're playing is like a bastard child that no one bothered to raise."

"Does everything with you have to be so damn serious?" she asks.

"Yes. I like my jazz. You can leave when you want." He points to the door.

Frank notices me.

"And who are you?" he asks.

"You Frank, right?" I ask.

"Depends who is asking."

"I work for Osiris Jones. My name is Paul."

The girl gets up and joins her friends who are rolling a joint on the top of a dresser.

"Osiris? I told him I'd get him the money. You're interrupting our study session."

I ponder what to say next.

"You can leave now," he says.

I don't move.

"Are we going to have a problem?" he says, holding up a personal alarm device with a flashing red L.E.D. that resembles a pager. "Because my security downstairs will be here with the push of a button."

"Security?" I ask.

"That's right. They may not look like much, but they get the job done."

"What do you pay them in?"

"What's it to you?"

"From the looks of it, I'm guessing steroids, maybe speed."

"What makes you say that?"

"Their temperament, their shakiness, and their pimply mugs . . . anything to keep them killing on the football field and pulling all-nighters. You've got some racket here, Frank. You supply what these kids demand. Smart."

"What did you say your name was?" he asks, glaring at me puzzled. "And how the hell did you get in here?"

"Relax. I'm no cop. It's like I said, I work for Osiris. Can we talk somewhere private?"

"What do we have to talk about?"

"The money you owe. It's best you pay up."

Frank studies me for a long moment, searching my face

for a quiver or a telling blink, but my face is convincing enough.

"I don't leave this room," he says, tapping his vile of coke against the coffee table. "Everything I have is in this room." He pours out a few more lines, dividing them with the edge of his platinum credit card.

"Can I sit?"

"I don't know," Frank counters. "Can you?"

I take a seat next to him on the tan lounge that matches the couch—something much too nice for college kids, even if they are Ivy League. I get a good look at Frank: he's pale, ratty, with a long pointy nose, crooked, like it's been broken and didn't heal straight. His front tooth is chipped and jagged. And he's greasy, like a fry cook.

"I'm going to need that money, Frank."

"I heard you the first time. Why didn't Osiris come get it himself?"

"He's busy."

"That's not what I heard. I heard the police are on him."

"Which is why it's best to keep the peace between you and him."

"Why is that?" he says. "If he goes down, I can easily buy from someone else to supply me."

"Have you ever been to prison, Frank?"

Frank shrugs.

"Well, Osiris has. I have. And I'll tell you, Frank. They would love you in prison—a white boy like you."

"Please, what is it with you people and these badges of honor for getting locked up? You know what the problem is with you people? You don't know how to be civilized."

"You people?" I ask.

"That's truly it," he says. "It's not that you do crime. I mean every ethnicity commits crimes. It's that you have to make such a spectacle of it when you do it. It's why it's so easy to lock up so many of you. You all should take a lesson from the Asians. Smart, smart criminals. They do it quietly."

"You want to watch your mouth, Frank?"

"See, we're right back to violence. I read a statistic once, that every seventy-two minutes a black person is killed by another black person. Nobody's killed people that fast since Hiroshima and Nagasaki. It's like you've forgotten your history. I mean if my people suffered how yours have . . . I mean slavery, then the Civil Rights Movement . . . the worst food, the worst housing . . . you would think that the weak gene line would have died off and a superior race of people would have emerged by now. But instead it's the opposite, like cockroaches. A small percentage has evolved while the majority has remained inferior and just sophisticated enough to walk, eat, and shit."

I want to drive my knuckles into his jaw. I had expected a wanna be, a white boy adorned in baggy pants and a sports jersey, making money off the rich kids, while emulating the gangsters and rappers on television. But instead I got an educated, jazz-loving bigot, a certified Ivy League racist, barely a step above a cellblock skinhead.

Frank sits confident because he's right. To cause a ruckus on his turf would only be the end of me. Even if I could make it past his frat boy security, the cops would be waiting outside by the time I made it to the front door. I'll have to keep my cool, play his game, wait till he gets bored and gives up the cash.

"And what about you, Frank?" I say. "Selling the same poison that put blacks in the yoke to your own people?"

"These people don't mean shit to me. I'm no rich kid. To them, I'm poor white trash on scholarship."

"Sounds like your own brand of social Darwinism."

"You've got it. This is social Darwinism at its best. Their weakness is dope. I supply it, get paid and educated at the same time. You know, you're much too smart to be working for Osiris."

"What do you think is going to happen if Osiris goes down?" I ask.

"Well, considering the current prison trend, he would have to kill someone or become . . . what's the phrase the kids use? Yes, someone's bitch."

"Let's back up, before he gets to prison," I say. "You would be the first person he would name. You're two years off a long bid."

"Please, he needs me. I'm the only one who could make money up here, untouched."

"Osiris doesn't need anybody. Besides, what's stopping one of these kids from ratting you out?"

"The one thing Osiris taught me that was worth hearing out—always know a bit about the people you deal with. I've got dirt on everybody in this room. Who cheated on their final exam and who *roofied* Suzie Q and left her with her panties around her ankles. Catholic girls and their back-alley abortions, Lacrosse-playing queers getting hand jobs in bathroom stalls. Hell, devout Muslims who eat pork barbecue. I know secrets some people would do anything to keep hidden. You see, Paul? People from this world have so much to lose. And don't for a minute think Osiris hasn't done his homework on you either."

"I've got no secrets."

"Maybe you just haven't thought them through yet. Besides, what does this have to do with you anyway? Where's Bear?"

"Bear?"

"The big black sucker who normally collects for him."

"Oh, right. Bear."

Frank snorts a line and then rests his head back, using his thumb to keep the powder and mucus from dripping. I take the opportunity to think of something clever to say.

"Bear got sent up," I say.

"What?" Frank asks.

"Something about failure to pay child support."

Frank laughs.

"Bear has children? Who the hell would lie down with him?"

I laugh with him, hoping to lighten the situation.

"So you're Bear's replacement?"

"Yes."

"You don't look like much. At least Bear was big."

Frank does another line and then pushes the small mirror toward me.

"Go ahead," he says.

"No. I'm good."

"I guess you're an exception to the rule."

Frank does another line and then props his feet up on the coffee table.

"So, about the money, are you going to pay what you owe?"

"I don't know," he says. "Let me think about it."

Frank snorts another line and then takes out a wad of bills. He sets the bills down on the table.

"Go ahead," he says. "Take the money."

I reach for the bills, and Frank snatches the money back like an obnoxious child.

"I thought you people are supposed to be fast."

I rise from the lounge and snatch Frank by his tie, wrapping it around my fist.

The room goes silent, and I find myself paying close

attention to the jazz music: The Herbert Hewitt Compilation, volume five.

I say: "You're a real comedian, you know that? I'll give you something to laugh about. . . ."

I wrap the tie around my fist again, stretching the fabric tight around his neck. His mouth is dry and his brow drips sweat. I turn to the thong girl who's shaking a bit. Her eyes are fixed on Frank.

"Now, I'm going to take the money you owe and walk out that door," I say, the veins around my temple protruding. "I'm not going to hurt you. Considering you're not thinking straight due to all that shit you put up your nose. But if you ever jump bad with me again, I'll make it so the only thing going up your nose will be a rubber tube."

Frank's eyes become watery, and I let go of his tie. He takes a deep breath and collapses on the couch. I quickly grab his personal alarm and send it flying across the room, crashing into the wall and then falling behind a bookshelf. I do a quick count of the money and then shove the wad into my pocket, which produces an unsightly bulge.

I turn to the thong girl.

"What's your name?" I ask.

"Christy," she says.

"You got a cigarette, Christy?"

Christy takes a pack from her back pocket and removes a smoke, handing it to me and then producing a lighter from the small coin pocket of her cutoffs.

"Thank you."

Christy smiles and lights my smoke. I head toward the door, leaving Frank speechless and reddened.

My hand is on the doorknob when Frank finally breaks his silence.

"Christy, get over here," he says.

Christy does as she's told, cowering like a scorned dog and pausing to look back at me.

"You like jazz, Frank?" I ask.

Frank clears his throat and attempts to deepen his voice, trying to sound as masculine as possible.

"The good stuff," he says.

"Me too, it's good music. Maybe you should think about giving this up, going straight. What's your major anyway?"

"Sociology, urban studies," he says.

I chuckle at the irony.

Outside the door I give a sigh of relief. The stairs are even more packed than before. I push past guys groping girls, girls kissing girls, kids passing joints. There's a group of boys at the front door taking turns sucking beer from a bucket with the aid of a cut garden hose. I move toward the kitchen figuring there's a back door, common in old Philly row houses.

The kitchen is just as packed as the rest of the house. A girl stripped down to her bra and wearing frayed jeans is lying on the counter. People take turns sprinkling salt on her stomach and then licking it up with their tongues. A boy places a lime wedge in her mouth and then forces his mouth onto hers. She gags some and then spits the lime out. She laughs while the boy's entourage cheers him on. At the end of the kitchen I see a door. I squeeze past a few girls who are passing around a bottle of cheap vodka and shouting at the top of their lungs, challenging each other to see who can drink the most. I'm a few feet away from my exit when Devon calls to me.

"Hey!" she shouts. "I guess we should have pinky swore."

She's a bit sweaty from dancing, still holding the same beer, the label worked over by her fingers and peeling from the moisture.

"Sorry," I say.

"Was Frank all you had hoped?"

I laugh. "You know Frank. He'll never change."

She moves in closer and my escape mission is cut short.

"So, is that dance out of the question?" she asks.

"I'm not much of a dancer. But I could use some fresh air."

"I'll join you. It's stuffy in here."

"Okay."

Once outside I can make small talk, tell her I'm too old for her and catch a cab.

"Not that way though," she says, pointing toward the backdoor. She exits the kitchen and I follow her until we reach the front door. The boys are still funneling beer, but move aside when she approaches. She turns around to make sure I'm still following, extending her hand for me to take. I do against my better judgment. The moment our flesh meets, one of the boys funneling beer nudges my shoulder with his elbow. I turn around, expecting an apology, or at least an "excuse me." But instead he moves closer, pressing his chest against me and squaring off like the precursor to a schoolyard brawl.

"Devon, who the hell is this guy?" he asks.

"We're just getting fresh air," I say.

I regret aligning myself with her because once I do his cheeks burn red and he puts the funnel down.

"God, Chase, will you relax?" she says, pulling my arm and fighting to get out of the door.

Chase gets in front of me, blocking my way. Every time I try to get past, he pushes me back. I size him up. He's about two inches taller than me with the body of a football player, maybe a tight end. He smells of cheap beer and even cheaper cologne.

"Come on, Chase, let him past," Devon says.

Devon looks at me and mouths *Sorry*.

I snatch the beer bottle from her hand.

Chase is too busy mocking me with his friends to notice I have the bottle emptied and raised. I wait for him to turn and face me. Our eyes meet, and I succumb to every emotion that involves sending the bottle into his face.

The bottle doesn't break. It stays solid. I hear a crack. His nostrils explode, sending blood onto my suit and other partygoers.

Devon screams.

The blood spray is heavy and for a moment I'm even stunned by the amount. It runs thick and dark, despite Chase's efforts to pinch off the valve.

"My nose!" he shouts. "The bastard broke my nose!"

The beefy boy with the backward cap comes in to investigate. He pulls his knife, but drops it once he sees the amount of blood flowing from Chase's nose.

"Chase?" he asks.

"Call an ambulance," he says, fighting not to swallow the blood.

"Shit!" the beefy boy says, making a run for the door. A partygoer shouts from behind me for people to get out. The crowd begins to scramble, most rushing for the back door and all avoiding the front. Once the front is clear, I walk out much easier than I came in.

Outside, I toss the beer bottle into the shrubs and quickly move away from the house. Minutes later, people pour out of the front door and quickly get on their cells, some struggling to snap shots of me with their camera phones. I pick up the pace, jogging toward the street, waving my hand at every cab that passes, desperate for a free one. I turn back to see a crying Devon being comforted by her girlfriends and a bleeding Chase holding his shirt to his nose, an erect middle finger his only protest. I smile satisfied, but don't allow myself true joy until a cabbie sitting at a red light signals for me to get in.

"Where to?" he asks.

"Center City, Walnut Street," I say.

The light turns green. I stay crouched down in the backseat and out of sight, until we get a good distance from the campus and make the turn onto Walnut.

"Rough night?" the cabbie asks.

"You don't know the half," I say, removing my blood-stained suit coat. "You know a good dry cleaner?"

"My brother-in-law, best in South Philly."

The cabbie hands me a coupon for 10% off a total dry cleaning bill at Moses' Dry Cleaning.

"The best in South Philly?" I ask.

"The best," he repeats.

When I arrive at the Royale, the night manager is just returning from his break with a cup of coffee and a hoagie from the 24-hour corner deli. I follow him up the stairs and into the lobby where he quickly moves behind the counter, sets his sandwich and coffee aside, and slides me a small piece of notepaper.

"This was left for you," he says.

The note reads: WE NEED TO TALK. MARCUS SAID YOU COULD HELP. The note is signed *Jasmine*.

"Did you see who left this?" I ask.

"Sure. It's the same girl whose been hanging out front for the last few days. I've threatened to call the cops on her, but she never budges. She's small, black, and jumpy, real jumpy. She just about finished that whole pot of coffee." He points to the day-old pot on the guest services table.

"When was she here?" I ask.

"Two hours ago. Maybe three."

I place the note in my pocket and begin to walk toward

the stairs that lead to my room.

"Look," he shouts, "I don't want any trouble here!"

"What makes you think I give a damn about what you want?" The manager is silent. "And give me a clean set of linen in the morning," I say, leaving the lobby before he has the chance to snap back.

Upstairs, I undress and climb into bed. I'm too tired to give the note much thought, but the manager did have a point. I don't want any more trouble either. I've got enough trouble, trouble to spare. If I don't pay the note any mind, maybe it'll just disappear.

I close my eyes and imagine the farm.

CHAPTER SEVEN

I AWAKE TO SEVERAL POUNDS on my door. When I answer, the manager is standing next to a white man with sandy brown hair and a scraggly beard. He's wearing a short-sleeve dress shirt without a tie and a pair of casual slacks. He removes his sunglasses to reveal his green eyes, chartreuse really and more reptilian than human. It only takes me a moment to recognize him and when I do a flood of emotions come rushing. His face is one I had hoped never to see again: Richard Moiye.

"I don't remember asking for a wake-up call," I say.

Moiye flashes his gold shield.

"Detective Richard Moiye," he says.

"What can I do for you, Detective?"

"I think you know."

I look to the manager whose face is a permanent haughty smile.

"That'll be all, sir," Moiye says to him.

When the manager doesn't move, Moiye gives him a slight nudge.

"Take a walk, buddy," he says a little wound up.

The manager shrugs and heads down the hallway looking back at me, as I stand unkempt in my boxer shorts.

"Put some clothes on," he says. "I'm taking you to the station."

"Am I under arrest?"

"I can arrest you if it'll make you feel better, but I thought we could just talk. I think you'll be interested in what I have to say."

I realize if he arrests me, he'll be sure to keep me in a holding cell for at least eight hours, and I simply can't afford to waste that kind of time. So I agree and throw on my suit slacks and a clean undershirt.

Outside, I rummage in my pocket and realize I left the GPS tracker in my pants. A panic sets in, and I wonder if I've signed my own death sentence. Moiye puts me in the back of his silver police sedan, something American with cheap navy interior. He slams the door shut and climbs in behind the wheel. He's fitter than I expected, of course older, but he's taken care of himself. Most Philly cops are overweight and sloppy, but Moiye looks strong. He sits with a straight back, his hands on the wheel at ten and two.

"Want the window down?" he asks.

"Please," I say. The window retracts halfway.

"As far as it goes," he says.

I knew Moiye would bring me in sooner or later, and I'm relieved he's getting it out of the way now. I'll probably spend a few hours going back and forth with him, telling him I have nothing to do with Osiris Jones, that I've never met the man, that I'm an ex-con turned businessman trying to get my life right, trying to make the best of my second chance—a second chance granted by the state of Pennsylvania and oh how grateful I am for their faith in me.

When we reach the station, I'm ushered down the hallway by a uniformed officer and then cuffed to the side of a table in the hot box. Moiye comes in minutes later with a stack of photos and a newspaper. He drops the *Daily Pennsylvanian* in front of me and takes a seat.

"Read the paper much?" he asks.

"I find the news depressing."

"Well, you're a bit of a local celebrity. You've made the paper."

"I don't follow."

"Page six."

I flip the page with my free hand. A column to the right reads WEST PHILADELPHIA CRIME SPILLS ONTO THE CAMPUS OF UPENN. Below is a small grainy photo of my back as I flee from last night's party.

"Since when does the *Daily Pennsylvanian* print on weekends?" I ask.

"Since thugs infiltrate college parties," he says. "They rushed the issue. Something about student safety. A student snapped the photo with his camera phone. We've been watching Webster for the past week. I wouldn't have paid the photo any mind had we not caught the reverse shot."

He drops a very clear black and white photo of me moving toward the taxicab. Chase and the brood of students are behind me, slightly out of focus, but enough to hold up in court.

"My surveillance team got a feeling you didn't belong and tailed your cab to the hotel. Talk about bad luck. You want to tell me what you were doing there?"

"I was invited," I say.

"That right?"

"Sure."

"A house full of Ivy League college kids say you assaulted the son of a Minnesota congressman with a beer bottle and accosted a girl in the entryway. The University City police wouldn't want anything more than for me to turn you over for a modern-day lynching."

"Then why didn't they pick me up?" I ask.

"Because there's something I need you for, Paul. I pulled your file and to tell you the truth, I owe you."

"Owe me for what?" I ask.

"Don't play dumb. I never forgot you, Paul, and I know you haven't forgotten me. You look different. You're older, tired—a bit rundown. But I couldn't forget you, even if I tried. Your case made me a detective—first-grade. You launched my career." He's beaming with accomplishment.

I throw the newspaper across the room, sending the print into the air and then raining down to the floor.

"Go to hell, Moiye!"

"You first."

"I want to make my phone call," I say.

"I haven't placed you under arrest. We're just talking remember?"

"I'm done talking."

"Fine, how about you just listen." He removes another stack of photos from his folder. They're snapshots of Osiris peering from his apartment window, getting into his van, meeting with other shady figures, and finally a snapshot of me leaving Osiris' apartment. Enough to put me back in for life.

"Being in consort with Osiris Jones is a parole violation," he says.

"I'm off parole," I say.

"In this city, you're never really off parole. Besides, with your fight at the party last night and those kids' statements, I'm sure it would be enough for some charges to stick."

"You ruined my life."

"I did? I wasn't the one who killed that woman, Paul, that poor woman and her little boy. What was he, six? Did I put a gun to your head and tell you to get behind the wheel drunk out of your mind? You did it on your own, Paul, all you. I've always wondered if I would see you again. I thought if anyone would learn from a mistake it would be you. But here we are. Again."

"What is it you want from me?"

"I want Osiris," he says, his eyes burning with ambition. The same look he delivered on the witness stand as he recounted the night I've fought to forget, the night I struck Martha Gibbons and her son, Albert. Moiye was the first responder and the story he told left the jury in sobs, and everything I had tried to keep, the life I had built—my job, my woman—collapsed in one frame.

I can still remember the sound of Martha Gibbons' body rolling off the hood of my '64 Dodge, the classic Dart, peeling gold paint and dented chrome. It had to feel like a bullet striking her. And her poor boy let out a cry that could make the coldest soul shudder, maybe even give the devil chills. He was dragged under the car, his face burned from the heat and exhaust, barely recognizable, limbs twisted, his body a heap of bones. In court, the coroner testified that a broken neck killed him—that had I just slowed down upon impact, he may have survived. But his mother was killed instantly, her mangled remains thrown twenty feet, everything turned inside out. They found her slumped among garbage and broken bottles, her skin scraped from her face and covered in blood.

"I can't help you," I say.

"Then it's back to prison," he says, affirming the obvious. "I'm just a worker."

"How did you get into business with him? If he has something on you, I can help. I can make a way for you."

"Make a way for me? You know the shit I'm in if anyone saw me dragged in here?"

Moiye gets in my face, breathing heavy.

"I know what Osiris is capable of," he says. "He's something without a conscience. I put him behind bars once and next time he'll die there, and he deserves to die for the things he's done."

Moiye pulls out more photos. This time parts of the images are covered with yellow sticky tags. Moiye removes the tags, and I nearly lose it from what I see. For a moment it doesn't look human. The charred body of a man, his genitals ravaged and blackened.

"He did this over a debt," Moiye says, and then removes another sticky tag from a smaller photo. This time it's a woman in her twenties, nude. She looks to be strangled.

"This is the man you work for, Paul. What type of man does these things?"

Moiye slides the final photo in front of me. I turn away. Moiye removes the sticky tag slowly.

"And this," he says, "his own mother."

It takes all my will and curiosity to look. It's a photo of an older woman, drug-worn with a hole in her head the size of a silver dollar, the thick contents oozing to a tiny heap just above her eyebrow.

"When was this taken?" I ask.

"Two days after he was released. She was supposed to be safely keeping a stash of money for him. Cash Osiris had amassed from drug sales. When he got out, she told him that she had spent it. So he killed her."

"How do you know?" I ask. "Osiris is more talk than anything."

"Talk? Does this look like talk to you?"

Moiye shoves the photo of Osiris' mother in my face. I push it away.

The images of the bodies mutilated in pools of blood and feces are still in my mind like a ghost image on an old television set.

"You're going to help me get him, Paul."

"The hell I am," I say defiantly.

"Then it's back inside," Moiye says. "I can have a judge sign the warrant today. Have you transferred in the morning. And don't think Osiris will come to your rescue, because he won't."

If I play along with Moiye, maybe he'll let me go. I can get Osiris his money and then leave for good.

"I won't wear a wire," I say.

"You won't have to. But we'll need solid intel about his apartment, like where he sleeps? How many guns he has inside? What's the best point of entry? And you'll need to testify in court."

"You're dreaming. I'll tell you what I know about the apartment, but I'm not testifying."

"We can protect you. Put you in WITSEC."

I laugh. "I'd never make it to the trial, no matter who you had watching my back."

"You don't have much of a choice, Paul," he says determinedly. "I will lock you up if I have to."

"For a moment, I actually thought all this was for Marcus Wallace. That somebody at least had him in mind. But who was I kidding?"

"Marcus is just the icing on the cake. Whether Osiris killed him or not, he's going down for it."

"And that's justice?"

"It's justice enough for Marcus, justice enough for the state of Pennsylvania, and justice enough for me."

"When do you move in on him?" I ask.

"We're monitoring him now. But it may be two or three days depending on what information you can give us."

Moiye keeps me at the station for about four hours. I give him details about the apartment, some accurate, but mostly lies. I tell him about a fictional room where Osiris sleeps, a sort of panic room with walls of reinforced steel. When Moiye bucks his eyes, I know I've overdone it and I pull back some with more feasible things about the apartment, like secret escape routes and booby-traps set in case of a raid. Moiye writes it all down and repeats that I'm doing the right thing. I could care less about Osiris, about Moiye, and at this point, about Marcus. I just want to get out of town.

Moiye lets me go once he's satisfied and drops me off at the hotel. He gets out and walks around to the rear passenger door and opens it. I stay seated.

"Osiris is going to know about this," I say. "He has dirty cops on the force."

"Sure. Coming from an ex-con, any cop who does their job is dirty."

"Tatum King."

"King?"

Moiye takes a moment to consider what I've told him. I can imagine that King's flamboyant suits and expensive watches pops into Moiye's head. I know he's at least partially considered what I've told him and that's good enough for me.

"They'll let him know we talked," I say. "But I have an idea. A way to convince Osiris I was quiet."

"You better not be pulling my leg," he says.

"I don't have the luxury. If I'm not careful, I'll end up in a photo covered with one of those goddamn sticky tags."

"Okay. So what do you want to do?"

"Sixth and Bainbridge. It's a garage."

Moiye shuts the door and gets back into the car. We head down an alleyway and take a sharp right and then two sharp lefts.

It takes me a moment to realize that Moiye is dry-cleaning in case we picked up a tail. He finally pulls the car into a parking garage after flashing his badge and getting waved through by the attendant. He parks the car in the most secluded spot he can find, between a minivan and an SUV.

"This will do," I say.

We get out of the car. Moiye removes his shirt. I stand there with my hands in my pockets as he approaches.

"So, how do you want it?" he asks.

"Anything, except the teeth."

The first blow he delivers is to my cheek and I nearly fall back, catching my balance on the side of the minivan. I cough up a chunk of blood and run my tongue around my mouth making sure my teeth are all in tack. The next blow is to my eye and it knocks me to the ground.

"Okay," I say, my palms smacking the pavement.

"You all right?" he asks, helping me up.

"I'll live."

"I didn't hurt you too bad, did I?"

It's the first time he's actually sounded concerned about my well-being. I can't help but laugh at the circumstance.

"You've got a strange sense of humor," he says, as he props me up against the SUV.

"In my dreams, I've always thought it would be the other way around. I'd be the one punching you."

"You know it doesn't have to be this way. I don't know

what Osiris has on you, but there's always a way out."

"I tried to get out and now I'm here with you. What does that tell you?"

"You still have a choice."

"Yeah, a choice," I say, mocking him and then spitting out more clots of blood.

"You've still got a future," he says. "As long as you're breathing, you still have a chance."

I spit again.

A future, a chance . . . the words alone are foreign. The concepts I can't begin to fathom. It's as if everything in my life has been leading up to these last few days, a predetermined fate sending me down a path that will tell what type of man I am. If there's anything left inside of me that's worth salvaging. Perhaps the hour is near? It's time for me to box with God. It's time for him to reckon with his mistake.

Moiye drops me off at the corner of 15th and Catherine. It takes me ten minutes to walk to Tammy's clinic. Before going into the clinic, I assess the damage to my face in a truck side mirror. I've been in worse shape.

I stumble through the sliding doors into the clinic. The check-in nurse approaches me holding a clipboard. She's thick, dark brown, with round hips and braids.

"Health coverage?" she asks.

"No."

She doesn't give me eye contact. Her pen is poised and she's holding the clipboard at an angle. She reminds me of a diner waitress taking an order.

"Known diseases?" she asks.

"None."

"What happened?"

"I was beaten."

She surveys my face, pausing to take notes.

"Physical altercation . . . doesn't look life threatening. It'll be about two hours." She hands me a number slip.

"Is there anyway I can see Tammy?"

"Tammy?"

She gives me a hard stare. It's been years and my face is battered, but she remembers.

"Paul?" she asks.

"Yes," I say, with a tinge of shame. The fact I'm here, looking as I do, only proves what so many at the clinic thought—that I'm worthless, good for nothing and no good for Tammy.

"What you want with Tammy?" she says, barely whispering. "I thought she put you out."

"I have to talk to her. Is she here?"

"She's about to go to lunch, but you're not supposed to be here, remember? They took a restraining order out on you."

I keep an eye out for Tammy's boss knowing that if he sees me, he'll be sure to call the cops and have me picked up.

"Yes," I say. "I know. But I'm hurt and I need Tammy."

"Look, you wait here and I'll see if she's in the back."

"Okay."

I take a seat in the busy lobby. There's a stack of old magazines and a trashy talk show on the television. Most people are too depressed and sick to care about what's on the TV. They look as if they're on the verge of giving up, like at any minute they would just lie down on the dusty laminate floor, look up to God and say *Take me, damn it! If you have half a heart, an ounce of compassion, take me!*

It's a feeling I understand.

Tammy appears from the hallway and slowly approaches me. I get up and move toward her. I can't read her. If she's still angry, she's hiding it well.

"Why are you here?" she asks.

It's like I haven't seen her in years. Her beauty assaults me.

159

"It's nice to see you, Tammy."

"Paul, what do you want?"

"I need medical attention."

"Yeah, I see that," she says, trying not to show too much concern.

I take her by the arm and usher her toward the hallway. A patient gets a glimpse of my number slip. There are at least twenty patients waiting in front of me.

"What the hell?" the patient says. "I've been here for an hour." He rises from his seat with the aid of his cane and throws his number slip to the floor.

"Relax, sir," Tammy says. "You will be called."

"You people are animals, you know that? Animals." He falls back into his seat.

I breeze past the reception desk and find a corner of hallway with the least foot traffic.

"You've got five minutes," she says.

"Tammy, I'm leaving. I'm going back to North Carolina."

"I have to get back to work."

Tammy turns away.

"I owe you something," I say.

"Brother, you owe me a lot," she says, shifting her weight to her right hip.

I take out a few bills from my pocket, a fifty, a twenty and some tens.

"Take this," I say.

"An apology will do," she says.

"Just take it."

"Why? So you can feel better about yourself? About how you did me wrong?"

"I can never pay you what I owe. But it's something, right?"

"Lord, Paul, you don't get it. I loved you. I still do

sometimes. I didn't take you in trying to save up for heaven. I took you in because I loved you. But you just can't be loved, can you? It's like no matter what good is in your life, you always find a way to ruin it. Well, you're not going to ruin me. I'm moving on and I suggest you do the same."

"Tammy, I'm begging you. Just take the money."

Tammy is silent. My hand is tight on her arm and I can't let go.

"When are you going to get yourself together? Look at you, a week without me and you look like hell. But this time you've got to deal, Paul. Whatever you've gotten yourself into, you've got to deal. Now leave before my boss sees you. He's never forgotten what you did to his arm and he's still bound to sue."

Tammy pulls her arm away and takes a first-aid kit from behind the nurses' station.

"I'm sorry," I say.

"Baby," she says, handing me the kit, "sometimes sorry ain't enough. I suggest you clean up those wounds, so they don't get infected."

The check-in nurse approaches.

"You okay, Tammy?" asks the nurse.

"I'm fine," Tammy says. "I'm going to lunch, Loretta. You want something?"

"Diet cola."

"Sure thing."

Tammy leaves me in the musty clinic and exits through the employee access to the rear parking deck. I tell myself if she looks back, she still cares. I watch her until I see her boss coming down the hallway in the distance. I don't risk waiting for her to look back. I walk out of the clinic, passing a sickly woman who is sweating heavily and is wrapped in a bed sheet. I give her my number slip.

At the hotel I get myself cleaned up the best I can with the first aid kit and washcloths. I know I won't heal well. Some of these scars may be for life. Everything about me seems to be changing. Inside, I'm not the same. I'm finding peace in the chaos. Something was quenched when I was serving Dougie his beating and now with Moiye, my heartbeat never wavered. I took the beating because I deserved it.

I put two hundred dollars of my cut of Osiris' money in my pocket. I place the eight hundred left in the safe, double-checking to make sure the lock isn't faulty. I don't trust Osiris enough to divvy up my share and it's best I take my cut up-front. I lie down for about thirty minutes to rest my eyes, when I hear a shallow knock at the door. I get up and look through the peephole, but all I see is empty hallway.

"Who is it?" I ask.

"Please, open the door. I need to talk to you." The voice is soft, faint, female.

I unlatch the chain lock, and I slowly pull the door open. Standing there is the genesis of my predicament. Her beady red coals looking back at me with an odd affinity. A rage comes over me that I can barely keep from boiling to the surface. All I can envision is the girl being on the receiving end of my fist.

"You Paul?" she asks, pushing past me wearing the same get-up she had on the night she climbed into my cab, but minus the blouse. The vest is covering up her goods like some outdated teen beat outfit and she's got barely enough meat to cover the bone. She looks like she hasn't slept and she's more than a few days past bathing. Her hair is still tinged with blood. She takes a seat on the corner of the mattress.

"So you're the guy Marcus went on about," she says.

"Is this some kind of joke?" I say. "You know full well who I am. If it weren't for you getting into that cab, I wouldn't still be in this damn city."

"What cab?" she asks.

"The one that took you to the hospital so you could get those stitches in your head."

"I was jumped. That's all I remember. Marcus said if something went wrong with the money I could find you here and that you could help."

"You're lying."

I take her by the arms, stand her up and push her against the wall so hard that she bumps her head against a picture frame and drops to the floor. I want to do the worst.

"Shit," she says, picking herself up, "what's your problem?"

"You're full of it. Get the hell out before I really hurt you."

"I've got no place to go," she says, on the verge of tears.

"Sorry for you. Now beat it before something bad happens to you."

"Paul, please. It's not what you think. I needed you. I still do."

"You set me up so I wouldn't leave town, hemmed me up with the cops. Bought yourself some time to find your way back here after you healed up."

"I had no choice. I've been watching this place, hoping you would be back. The manager said you were still hanging around, so I waited."

"How did you know it was me in the cab?" I ask.

"Marcus said to look for the green military bag. When I saw it, I just knew it was you and I couldn't let you leave town. I was watching you get into the cab when I was attacked. It was the men Marcus ripped off. I know it. I managed to get away, but I know they're coming for me and I think they may have killed Marcus."

I take a seat on the bed.

"So he took the package?" I ask.

"It was cash," she says. "About a hundred thousand dollars."

"Christ, he was some kind of stupid."

"Don't talk about Marcus like that. He did it for me. I'm pregnant. We were trying to get out of town, but they must have got to him before—"

"I hate to be the bearer of bad news, but Marcus had a fiancée, Shaina, and she's carrying his kid."

Jasmine brushes her hair from her shoulders in an almost comical attempt to spruce herself up. Perhaps at one time she was a catch. But that seems like ages ago.

"He was going to leave them," she says.

"And run away with you?"

"Why is that so hard to believe? We were in love."

"I don't know anything about that and I don't want to know. There's only one thing you can do for me. Tell me who killed him. Who did it, Jasmine? You've got to have some idea."

"I'm not sure," she says. "It could have been these men who attacked me or they could have hired someone to do it. All we wanted was to be a family. Marcus said it was risky, but I convinced him the money was the only way out. When he went missing, I feared the worst. So I went looking for the address he left with your name on it. I was about to go into the hotel when I was jumped. I need you, Paul. I need you to protect me."

"Where is the money now?"

"It was on him the night he died."

"Were you with him that night?"

"He told me to wait for him on Broad Street, but he never showed up. I think whoever killed him thinks I know where the cash is. That's why they roughed me up."

"Why didn't they kill you too?"

"They must have gotten scared off. Or maybe they figured I'd lie there and bleed to death. How the hell should I know?"

"And you're saying you didn't see these men?" I ask. "You can't tell me what they looked like?"

"It's like I told you, I couldn't make out their faces. I wish I knew, but it's all a blur."

"Just go to the police, Jasmine, and leave me be," I say, exhausted from the whole ordeal.

"I'm only asking for a few hours. I'm pregnant. I don't stand a chance out there."

"Well, you're still alive," I say. "You've made it this far."

I get up and head toward the door, prepared to push her out if need be.

"Please, Paul," she says, rubbing her belly, "I'm begging you. I can't go anywhere else. I'll be safe here. Just let me stay a few hours and then I'll leave."

I want to tell Jasmine to get lost and to take all her troubles with her. But I can't. If she is carrying Marcus' child, I should at least try and get her to safety. After all, Shaina and Jasmine's babies never asked to come into this world, but since they are, they at least deserve a fighting chance.

I tell her she can stay a few hours, but she has to leave when I get back. I agree to put her in a cab to the police station if she wants, but that's the limit of my benevolence. She gets cleaned up and then burrows into the sheets.

"Don't open the door for anybody," I say. "When did you eat last?"

"I don't know," she says.

"Well, that can't be good for the baby."

"It's not."

"I'll pick something up."

"Thank you."

I put on the soiled suit coat, place my book in my

waistband, and look at myself in the bathroom mirror to make sure my wounds aren't bleeding.

"What's with the book?" she asks.

"It's philosophy, David Hume."

"You look like you would read something like that," she says.

"What's that supposed to mean? What do you read? That is, if you even do?"

"I read. Magazines and stuff."

"I'm not surprised."

My tone is sharp and sarcastic. Jasmine takes offense.

"Well, try not to get your ass kicked this time," she says, with a crooked grin.

"Whatever."

Outside the hotel, the sun is low to the horizon. My face is aching and I'm short on sleep. Everything feels like a perpetual haze, a dream . . . a nightmare.

But there is an end. I'm close. I can feel it. All I have to do is give Osiris his money and get to the bus station. Moiye goes after Osiris. Tammy goes back to her life without me, and I return to the cradle of my grandfather's farm where I can finally be at peace.

CHAPTER EIGHT

IT TAKES ME THIRTY MINUTES to get to Osiris' apartment. When I arrive, he's visibly annoyed, exercising his trigger finger like a tic caused by Tourettes, moving it forward and back, and chewing his lip between curses.

"I told you that damn GPS wasn't for show. Didn't I warn you about the police?" He presses the gun to my cheek.

"I can explain," I say.

"If you brought the cops here, you'll be dead before they bust that door down," he says pulling back the hammer.

"I didn't talk. Why do you think I look like this?"

"The cops did that?"

"Yes, when I wouldn't talk, they roughed me up."

"Moiye isn't known for that."

"It wasn't Moiye. It was Tatum King."

Osiris considers what I've told him.

"I find out that you're lying and I'm going to make you

pay," he says, lowering the gun.

"You think if I was working with the cops, I'd come back here?"

I reach into my pocket and hand Osiris a bundle of bills.

"I took my cut already," I say.

Osiris takes a seat and places the bills in a counting machine and waits.

"Looks like it's all here," he says, as the machine finishes counting the last few bills.

"I doubt Frank would skim you," I say. "He's not that stupid."

"And I guess neither are you."

I didn't take the time to count it before, but there's at least fifty thousand dollars, minus my cut.

"We done?" I ask.

"Yeah, we're done," he says.

"What about the suit?"

Osiris gets up and inspects the suit, noticing the blood splatter on the sleeve.

"What is that?" he asks.

"Blood."

"Keep it. It looks better on you anyway."

"And the phone and GPS?"

"The phone is yours, but I'll need that GPS."

I remove the GPS tracker from the suit pocket and hand it to him.

"What about the book?" I ask, taking it from my waistband and handing it to him.

"How far along did you get?" he asks.

"Man and Justice," I say.

"That shit is too heavy for me. The Science of Man, more like the science of a dead man, because that's how you'd end up living by his rules in these streets."

"I guess a man has to make his own rules, his own science," I say.

Osiris thinks for a moment, flipping through the pages of the book.

"Go ahead, keep it."

"Thanks."

"You didn't do too badly, Paul. Maybe you've found your calling."

"Like I told you before, I'm no debt collector."

"It's just a suggestion, brother, just a suggestion."

"I'm not your brother either," I say coldly.

I leave Osiris sitting at the card table organizing his bills by president's faces. Outside, I see two cops sitting in a white 4-door SUV with a communication antenna mounted on the roof. They watch me, but don't act. I assume Moiye has given them the word I'm *working* on their side.

The suit has gone sour. Now that the job is done, I can ditch it for something more comfortable. I walk south to the Army surplus store on lower Walnut. I buy a pair of cargo pants and two T-shirts, one brown and another black. I get changed in a restroom at a fast-food restaurant and dump the suit in the garbage.

I stop at a pizza parlor on South Street and pick up a large pie and two side salads. The walk back to the Royale Hotel is a long one. On the way I see a group of brothers getting heckled by the police, legs spread with their fingers inner-locked behind their heads. A block later I see a suited man: drunk, disorderly, and screaming into a cell phone. At the next alley, two lovers are braced against a brick building, groping each other with no qualms about their public display affection. Perhaps these are the things that make this city what it is. Maybe the lack of decorum and depravity is all part of its charm.

When I arrive at the hotel, Jasmine is just waking from her

nap. I let her yawn and get acclimated to the land of living. She slept so hard she forgot where she was—she's jumpy, and eyes me like a stranger.

"I have dinner," I say.

"Umm dinner," she says, wiping the sleep from her eyes.

She gets out of bed, prances around, singing a soulful ballad, and then goes into the bathroom.

"What's that song?" I ask.

She stops singing.

"Just something I wrote," she says.

"Is that what you want to be, a singer?"

"I am a singer, just one that hasn't been discovered yet. But I'm going to New York and there everything is going to be perfect."

"And your baby?"

"My mother said she'll care for it."

I take a slice of pizza from the box and begin to eat. Jasmine joins me at the small mahogany table. She's in her panties and wrapped in a blanket that barely covers her breasts.

I try to keep my eyes on my pizza.

"After we eat, I'll put you in a cab," I say. "You're going to the police."

"Where are you going?" she asks.

"The bus station, I'm leaving here."

"The cops won't help me, you know that."

"I'll leave you in good hands. A detective I know."

Jasmine sighs disagreeably.

"Or you can hang around town and risk getting killed, but I'm done helping you," I say. "After this, you're on your own."

There's a knock at the door. I dread looking through the peephole expecting to see Moiye, the manager, or a possible tail Jasmine picked up.

"Keep quiet," I say to Jasmine, who's crouched down, expecting gunfire.

There's another knock. I realize it's too light a knock to be a man and the chance of gunfire is slim.

I glimpse through the peephole and see Kim. Eager to see her in the flesh, I swing the door open.

"Kim?"

"Don't look so surprised," she says.

"I just didn't expect to see you," I say. "But I'm pleased you came back."

"Are you all right? What happened to your face?"

"Long story."

"I'll have to hear it sometime."

I stand in the doorway, hoping my body language lets her know it's a bad time.

"I don't want to keep you," she says. "I just wanted to drop this off." She hands me a brochure about a dance performance.

"It'll be my last performance here in the city. I'm leaving for London in a few days and I thought you could come see me dance. Maybe we can get dinner after?"

The night we spent together is thick in the air. I want to tell her I'll be there, front row, but I option for a gentler lie.

"I'll try to make it," I say.

"Well, if you can. It would mean a lot to me."

Jasmine begins to hum the tune again. Kim hears it and begins to rubberneck over my shoulder.

"You have company?" she asks.

"Just watching over a friend," I say.

Jasmine's humming turns into singing. She gets progressively louder and then stops.

"You got anything to drink, Paul?" Jasmine asks. "I'm thirsty."

Jasmine gets up and heads toward the bathroom to get some water. Kim catches a glimpse of her and her olive skin turns ghostly white.

"Jesus, Paul," she says. "A bit young, don't you think? I knew it was a mistake coming here." She turns and rushes down the hallway. This time I take off after her.

"Kim, wait!"

"Save it, Paul. I knew you had issues. I mean, who doesn't? But is this your hustle? Get a hotel room, tell girls you're between living situations, and screw them?"

"No. It's nothing like that. She needs my help."

"Yeah, I'm sure. Goodbye, Paul. Have a nice life." She continues down the hallway as fast as her legs will allow.

I whisper goodbye and watch her until she's gone. I walk back into the room. Jasmine is putting on her skirt, her backside exposed without shame.

"Who was that?" she asks.

"Nobody."

"We going now?" she asks.

"Just let me get cleaned up."

There isn't time to grieve Kim's leaving. She's a bitter dream, a once beautiful thought that made me warm inside. But sooner or later I would have disappointed her. I would have shown her my true colors and sent her running for the hills.

Jasmine finishes getting dressed and goes back to eating pizza. I take a long shower, allowing the hot water to wash over my body. I scrub with soap twice. The cleaner I can get the better my chances are at fighting the thirteen-hour bus stench. I wash my hair with the tiny bottle of complimentary shampoo and then I apply a tea tree conditioner. I stay in the shower long enough for the hot water to run lukewarm.

I get out and towel off. I dry my hair and brush my teeth.

The bathroom is too steamy for me to shave, so I crack the door some. When I do, I notice Jasmine isn't sitting at the table. The pizza box with the half eaten pizza hasn't moved and the salad is untouched.

The room is empty. The mattress is flipped over and the dresser drawers are thrown about. I quickly check the safe. It doesn't open. The lock doesn't look tampered with, but I need to be sure. I remove the key from my cargo pants that are lying on the bathroom floor and open the safe. When I do, my chest pounds and I struggle to breathe. The money is gone.

I wish for a heart attack. I wish for God to take me, and before I give it much thought I send the empty safe crashing to the floor. I'm past irrational. I'm a goddamned madman with only one thing on my mind—I've got to get my money back.

My wallet and all the money I have left are in my cargo pants. I hastily put them on, along with my T-shirt and boots. I charge out of the room, leaving my book, toiletries, and anything else that's secondary in importance to the money behind. I rush down the hallway looking for Jasmine. I check the vending room, the fire escape, and the roof access. But there's no sign of her.

When I reach the lobby, I'm out of breath and the manager is on the phone.

"Where did she go?" I ask.

He ignores me.

I ask again, leaning over the counter so he's sure to hear. He puts his hand over the phone receiver.

"I'm on the phone with a customer," he says smugly. "You'll have wait."

"The girl, where did she go?"

"Are you deaf? I said, I'm on the phone."

I snatch the phone out of his hand and slam it down on the hook.

"What the hell is wrong with you? Do I need to get security?"

"No. You're going to need an ambulance unless you tell me what happened to the girl."

"What the hell are you talking about?"

"The girl who left the note. Fair-skinned, short. Did she leave here?"

He stares blankly.

"Damn it! Did she leave here?"

"She came down here about thirty minutes ago. I gave her the safe key. I was gone for a few minutes and when I came back the key was sitting on the counter."

"What safe key?"

He repeats, this time speaking slower as if I'm mentally handicapped or hard of hearing, "She needed an extra safe key. She said you misplaced it or something. I keep a spare here at the desk, but it's still going to be a ten-dollar replacement fee, hotel policy."

I strike him so hard that his tooth drives into the skin of my knuckle and grazes the bone. I wince from the pain, but it doesn't slow me down. I deliver another blow, this time to his chin, sending him to the floor. He struggles to get to his feet, leaning on the counter for support and bucketing tears. His cheek swells to the size of a baseball and turns a deep purple. His body is going limp. He's shaking at his base. His knees are unable to handle the strain and he drops to the floor with a thud, taking papers, a stapler, and a small potted plant with him.

I can't return to room 207. He spoke of security. He might have been bluffing. I've never seen more than a night watchman with a flashlight, but it isn't worth finding out. I sacrifice my belongings and David Hume's journal. I leave the Royale Hotel.

And this time I leave for good.

CHAPTER NINE

I SPRINT TO THE CORNER of Walnut and 15th Street, getting as far away from the hotel as I can before hopping in a cab. The traffic is dense and it takes twenty minutes to get halfway down Jefferson and in the vicinity of the Greyhound station. No matter how much money I dangle in front of the cabbie as an incentive to get me there faster, his hands are tied and it just frustrates him. So I sit still and keep quiet.

I'm down to one hundred and ninety one dollars and sixty-eight cents, the little bit of cash I had in my pants. When we arrive at the Greyhound Station, the cabbie looks relieved to let me out. I tip him two bucks, which is less than what he expected. He barely gives me enough time to shut the door before speeding off.

Inside, the station is outdated and smells of musty travelers. The seats in the lobby near the window are so old that the blue plastic has faded from the sun, making them two

176

shades lighter than the rest. I check the charter schedule. The next bus going to North Carolina is headed to Greensboro, a city nearly an hour away from my grandfather's farm. I stand in line for about two minutes until I'm called to the window. The attendant is eating peanuts from a small snack bag, and her red hair is shoved under a dirty knit cap with a blue visor.

"Any charters going to Mocksville, North Carolina?" I ask.

"Mocksville?"

She takes a moment looking at her computer.

"Sure," she says. "Tomorrow at three-thirty in the afternoon."

"That's too late," I say.

"Sorry. That's all we got. We have one headed to Greensboro in about an hour."

"Okay. That'll have to do. Give me a one-way."

"All right, window or aisle?"

"Window."

"Eighty dollars and sixty-five cents," she says.

I hand her the cash and she deposits it in the register. She hands me my change.

I thank her and take my ticket.

I have a seat in the lobby facing the television that is showing the evening news. I can barely keep my eyes open. The day's ordeal has left me spent. My head is pounding from the beating Moiye gave me and I'm worried about the hotel's security camera catching my midday battering. It'll take the manager all day to file charges against me and by the time the A.P.B. is issued, I'll be on my bus. I reassure myself over and over with a mantra: *Nothing is standing in my way. Nothing is stopping me from getting on this bus.*

Short of Moiye coming into this station with guns blazing and a warrant for my arrest, I'm leaving Philadelphia for good.

The sun is beginning to set as I watch travelers come and go from the station. I get a soda from the vending machine with the few coins in my pocket. The only thing left is cola, which I regret drinking because the caffeine is bound to keep me awake on the bus. I flip through an old copy of Philadelphia Weekly, periodically glancing at the news program. A live newsflash cuts into the typical broadcast of crime, rising gas prices, and the weather report.

I recognize Tammy's street as a reporter stands in front of her brownstone, swarming with blue suits and paramedics. I get up and move closer to the television in order to better hear. The reporter announces that an hour ago shots had been fired in the building, and that one person has been reported dead. I turn up the volume.

"Sir, please don't do that," the attendant says peering from behind the window. "You'll disturb the other travelers."

I look around the nearly empty Greyhound station. A few people are sleeping, but most of those in the station are homeless, hassling folks for money.

"What people?" I say. "No one is here."

I go back to watching. There is no mistake. It's Tammy's brownstone. Every horrific thought imaginable seems to bombard my consciousness at once. What if I jeopardized Tammy's life? What if the men who put Marcus in the grave went after Tammy? What if I led them to her, right to the clinic? They could have followed her home after work and had their way with her, asking questions about me, like my whereabouts, who I work for. Tammy wouldn't have known the answers. Outside of me planning to leave town, she wouldn't have had anything to give up, nothing to barter her life with, and then, maybe when they tired of her, they put a bullet in her cold.

A vision of Tammy lying on the kitchen floor overpowers all other thoughts. I see a pool of blood, thick, seeping through the floorboards and down to the first floor apartment. The crime scene cops are taking photos, sliding her body into a bag, her hands turning cold and stiff. I can see it so real. It fuels the fire in my gut. It's burning so hot that it borders on combustion, so that ash and bone would be all that would remain of me.

If Tammy is dead over the dirt I've done, I'm prepared to take the culprit's life and then my own. There wouldn't be enough tears to cry, enough prayers for forgiveness, enough sins to pay for to make it right. Nothing anyone could say could rid me of a pain like that. Death would be the only choice—the only viable amnesty, and I would go gladly.

A sickness comes over me, and I lose it in a trash bin sitting next to the soda machine.

"Sir, are you all right?" The attendant asks.

"No," I say, wiping my mouth with my T-shirt and trying to keep the vomit down.

"I want to refund my ticket," I say.

"A refund? But that bus will be here in fifteen minutes."

"I realize that. Please, just refund my ticket."

"Okay, sir. Okay." She takes the ticket and then plucks away at the computer. I glance back at the news. More cops have arrived and they've set up a perimeter with caution tape to keep the crowd back.

"Jesus Christ," I say.

"You going to be all right?" she asks.

"I will be as soon as you give me my damn money back!"

The attendant quickly finishes the transaction and slides me my refund, slamming the change down on the counter.

"Look, I'm sorry," I say. "I am."

"Yes. You sure are. Now go on. Get out of here." She points to the exit.

I pocket my money and sprint out of the station, dodging

bums, travelers, and station attendants.

Outside, I don't wait for a cab. I sprint up the block, running in the street and alongside cars in order to avoid people walking slowly on the sidewalk. I run until my chest feels like it's about to burst or cave in. I run until my muscles seize and tighten, until my shin splints flare, throb, and burn. I run powered by the prospect of Tammy's death. I run as tears swell in the corners of my eyes and stream down my face, and then I run some more.

In my mind I struggle to prepare myself for Tammy's death. I fight to build an emotional shock absorber, a way to stomach the pain, if only for a time, long enough to enact justice on her killer and then take my own life. I prepare my obituary. The words are to be simple: Let it be known that I existed. Paul Little lived. He breathed the same air as men, walked the same streets, ate the same food, but he could not be confused with a man. Inside he was nothing, nothing that resembled a human being, a new beast—a wretched thing, but real. He left the world as he came into it. In a barrage of violent acts that laid a foundation and made a way for a beast like him to be born and eventually ruined.

Who would commit my remains to the soil? I have no one left. My body would be left unclaimed in a morgue, or perhaps used for science, to be studied and understood by educated minds, but what of my soul? Is it to be launched into oblivion, carrying the weight of all my life's regrets, heavy enough for eternity?

When I reach Tammy's brownstone, I'm coughing so hard that I think I'm bound to die before I know the truth about what occurred. I grip my knees and concentrate on slow, steady, deep breaths. I fight the urge to panic, looking at the ambulance, the police, and the crowd that has formed. I push my way through the people, barely slowing down for the young children watching, licking popsicles, and eating ice cream cones. I break through as an unrelenting force. Finally, I reach an officer who presses his hand against my chest once he sees that the plastic caution tape is not going to stop me.

"Easy, pal," he says.

"This is my girlfriend's place," I say. "I live here."

"Well, you can't go up. It's a crime scene."

"Where is she? Is she all right?"

"Maybe you should wait here," he says. "I'll get a detective." He begins to walk away. I grab his arm and his jaw clenches.

"Fella, you don't want to do that," he says.

"Please, just tell me. Is she dead? Is Tammy dead?"

The officer removes my hand from his arm slowly, but with force.

"I can't bear to go up there and see her. I can't do it. Do you understand what I'm saying?"

"I understand. No woman was killed. You've got it backward. Tammy, you say?"

"Yes, Tammy Delgado."

The officer pauses, allowing the name to register.

"Yes, she's fine," he says. "She's getting checked out and then they're taking her down to the station. It looks like self-defense, but that's all I know. Come with me and you can talk to the lead detective."

I follow him past the barricade toward an ambulance where they are loading a body into the back. It's zipped in a body bag.

Tammy is sitting on the curb, taking slow sips from a cup of water, her mascara like two poorly drawn lines extending below her jawbone. Her face is drained of its color. She's peaked, indistinct. I hardly recognize her. Something has changed about her, her physiology. It's like looking at stranger. Her tank top is splattered with blood and her hair is covering her brow; it's positioned like a curtain over her face. She finally looks up, brushing her hair back to reveal her eyes, the windows into her unimaginable ordeal. Her face is washed in fear and rage. I recognize the signs. It's something I've seen before. Tammy looks like an inmate who has survived a prison yard brawl or an attempted gang rape. She's fought to preserve her humanity and in the wake of that she's taken a life. I now know it wasn't Tammy who hexed me when I walked out. It was me who put a hex on her. I caused this. Whatever happened here, I am responsible. She's been right all along. I have been robbing her of her sweetness, slowly, bit by bit. I've taken away her lovable spirit and now she's experienced something so horrific, so severe that there's no going back.

I approach her slowly and extend my hand. She takes hold of it and I help her up. We embrace tightly. I can't remember the last time I've held Tammy like this, so close I can hear her heartbeat. It's loud, fast.

"Paul, how did it come to this?" she asks, her voice crackly and soft. "How did this all happen?"

"I don't know," I say. "Sometimes we just aren't in control of things the way we think we are."

The words are as hollow as I am inside. I know how this all happened. It's been a domino effect. A string of events set into motion beginning with the moment I walked out of Tammy's apartment and left for good. I tipped the first domino into play and since then it's been toppling other pieces until it's finally completed, a masterpiece only God can comprehend.

"I'm so sorry," I say. "I really am."

"It happened so fast. He kicked in the door. There I was in

my bedroom. At first I thought it was you. Angry about the way I treated you at the clinic, drunk maybe."

"Tammy, I would never . . ."

"I know. But it's what came to me. Or maybe I was just hoping you loved me enough to kick down that door, like you were coming to work things out. No matter what."

"It was my grandfather's gun, wasn't it?"

"Yes. There it was in the closet with the things you left behind. I didn't think it was loaded. I thought I could just scare him away. But there was one bullet in the chamber and when I fired he just dropped." Her eyes drift off into nothingness.

"Who was it?" I ask. "What did he look like?"

A heavy hand finds its home on my shoulder and I turn around to see Moiye, hidden behind his sunglasses and holding a notepad.

"She shot Osiris," he says, calmly.

"Osiris? But how? I don't understand."

"She shot him with a rusty forty-five and good aim. She got him dead in the chest. It stopped him cold."

"But why would he come after her?"

"I was hoping you would have the answer to that question. Did things go wrong between you and him? How did your business end, Paul?"

"He was in good shape when I left him," I say.

"So now you admit you were working for him?"

Moiye jots a few notes on his pad.

"Yes."

"Are you prepared to give a statement back at the station?"

"I'll tell you whatever you want to know," I say, holding Tammy's hand. "It's over now."

She's in a daze, hardly aware of her surroundings and I'm grateful for it. At least God got that right. He gave us a shutdown switch, a way to checkout when things get too heavy. A paramedic comes over and takes her by the arm and walks her to the medical unit.

"She's not going to be all right, is she?" I say.

"No, Paul, she isn't," he says, preparing to walk away. "An officer will take you to the station. I have to wrap things up here."

"Moiye?"

He turns around and removes his sunglasses, his green eyes penetrating into the heart of whatever I am.

"What is it, Paul?"

"I never meant for this to happen. I need you to know that. I never would have put Tammy in danger. Things just got out of control."

"Yes, they did and now a man is dead. Maybe he had it coming, but Tammy pulled the trigger. That poor girl killed someone. That's something that just doesn't go away. But you already know that, don't you?" Moiye slips his sunglass back on and walks away.

The neighbors and building tenants are giving statements to the officers. They point and stare in my direction. I can only imagine what they are telling the police: "It's all that ex-con's fault. He brought this violence into our building— to our doorsteps. Lock him in a cell for life. Give him the chair. Hell, give him a firing squad!"

But even a firing squad wouldn't be justice enough for Tammy. Short of an eternity of torment, there is nothing that can make things right. North Carolina is a dream. My fate is here in Philly. I've boxed with God and there's no beating God. Maybe I was his experiment, God's own punching bag. A way for him to release the hate and frustration he holds for humanity without killing the whole lot of us—he picked me, the weakest and the most disposable to punish. I'm his crash dummy. He's sending me through peril like Job, only my peril is compassionless. God offers no reprieve. In the end, he won't repent for what he's done, because this isn't a test. This is the real thing and the only thing God repents for is hacking me into existence. I wish for him to strike me down, to suck the life right out of me. But he doesn't, and moments later an officer cuffs me and escorts me to a patrol car.

CHAPTER TEN

AT THE STATION I'M PUT BACK in the hot box. The station sergeant and a few other detectives come in to question me—nothing specific to the crimes and mostly about Osiris. Seeing as I was the last person to have worked for him, they treat me like a celebrity of sorts. They tell stories about him, as if he were some mythological being or a legend in urban folklore. They ask me what he was like in his last days. Then they bask in the complete irony of his death. Osiris, Philadelphia's most feared street king, murdered by a woman who had never fired a gun. The magic bullet, an officer remarks snidely. They revel in his demise.

I don't feel sorry for Osiris. I can't possibly feel anything toward him except contempt. But as another black man, as a product of this street ecology, I pity him. Who will bury a man like Osiris? Nobody will. No one will mourn him just as no one would mourn me. Journalists and reporters will advance their careers with exposés about him. Retired police will write books. Seasoned gangsters will preach of his downfall to stick up kids and hustlers. Osiris Jones, the last of the real gangsters, taken out by a single bullet to the heart.

There's something viciously poetic about it all. I became the sickness that infected Tammy, Osiris, even Marcus; leaving a lingering vapor trail I poisoned them all. So ready the prison cell. I'm prepared for my sentence. I will plead guilty to all crimes across the board. And when the prison lights go out, it will be the faces of those I've hurt that will haunt my dreams.

Moiye enters the room, holding a small tin box containing my wallet, my cash, and my acquired cell phone. He sets the box on the table and then removes the phone.

"You really should learn to check your voicemail," he says.

"I don't know much about cell phones," I say. "This was my first."

Moiye picks up the phone and dials. He puts the phone to his ear and then puts it to mine.

"Listen," he orders.

At first all I can do is make out Osiris' screeching voice, then a barrage of curse words, and finally the clearest part of the message: "You thought you could give me up to the cops? I told you not to cross me. I told you if you went to the cops I'd make you suffer. So I'm paying a visit to your little girlfriend. Think of this as a going away present."

The message ends, and I draw away from the phone. I want to smash it against the brick wall of the hot box, but I direct my anger at Moiye.

"It's your fault! I told you Osiris had a rat in this precinct! How else would he know?"

"You sent me on a wild goose chase with King. You can't have I.A.B. open a file on a cop and expect others not to scatter."

"If it weren't for you picking me up, none of this would have happened. Tammy could be home cooking dinner right now."

"Tammy was attacked because you decided to work for a psychopath. Osiris had it all mapped out. Every move you made linked to the GPS on his phone."

"I know that. The beating you gave me was supposed to sell him on the idea I didn't talk."

"Well, it didn't work," he says. "He must have gotten word we were going to move on him. We will find the rat."

"I don't care about the damn rat. I want to know how he knew where she lived."

Moiye removes a sheet of paper with printed phone numbers on it. "Phone records," he says.

He points to the last number on the sheet.

"Osiris made two phone calls before he died. The first was to you and the other to a Dooney's Barbershop in South Philly. Do you know someone at this location?"

There are only two people who could have possibly known Tammy's address: Dooney and Dougie. Dougie betrayed me once. It wouldn't be much of a surprise if he betrayed me again, but a call to the barbershop from Osiris' cell phone after hours? The thought of Dooney being involved in this is something I don't want to believe. Dooney is my friend, more like a father. Is it possible to go most of your life thinking you know someone and then finding out you never did? I suppose that's how Tammy felt about me. What would Dooney gain by helping Osiris? Osiris, who didn't have a pot to piss in, couldn't have offered up enough cash for Dooney. But what price could he put on betrayal?

I can't be locked away in a prison cell. Not now. Not with this hanging over me. A missing puzzle piece, the one thing that can finally help make sense is Dooney's barbershop. It was Dooney who pushed the businessman job on me in the first place. Could they have both been in cahoots together? But why, what would be gained making me the businessman's gopher? And what was the money for that Marcus stole?

I've got to get out of here.

"Paul?" he says.

My mind is racing, playing back all the events of the past few days.

"Paul?" he says again, with a pointed tone.

"What?!"

"I lose you for a second?"

"The answer is no."

"Paul, we know about this place. It's a front for illegal activity. Is it possible that someone here could have told him about Tammy?"

"I don't know a thing about it."

"You say you care about her. But you're not even willing to help us find out who gave her up."

"I take it back," I say. "I'm not giving a statement about anything. If you're going to charge me, then do it already."

"Charge you? No D.A. is going to take the time to prosecute Osiris' last living henchmen. You don't matter now that Osiris is dead. His organization is finished. Besides, what exactly are you guilty of?"

"What do you mean the last living?"

"New Jersey police found Bear dead in an alley. Osiris' signature was all over it."

"You mean the pool stick?" I ask.

"Yes, his calling card. We figure he got word Bear was cutting a deal over some pending drug charges. As you say, Osiris had eyes and ears everywhere. Osiris drove into Newark and took care of Bear. He probably would have gotten to you if he weren't short on time. His van was packed up with everything a person would need to survive on the run. But he just couldn't let it slide knowing you talked to me. So he went after Tammy instead. Truth is, had he not gone after Tammy he might have made it out of the city and headed down to Mexico by now."

"I thought you were supposed to be watching him."

"Osiris had the surveillance down like clockwork. In his apartment we found charts and schedules on our shift rotations, timed right down to the minute. We think he slipped out during the changing of the guard. We'll make Osiris for Marcus and Bear's murders. As for you, if you're smart, you'll leave this city and never come back. But then again, you haven't proven to be very smart."

"How do you know Osiris killed Marcus?"

Moiye laughs.

"You won't believe it, the last honest guy in the city. A cab driver shows up here this morning with a duffle bag and a wad of money. Says some guy left it in his cab. Turns out, inside the duffle bag were bills botched with blood and a piece of paper with Marcus' phone number jotted on it. I'm sure he had debated turning the money in, but bloody cash is bloody cash. On a hunch I sent the bills down to the lab for a preliminary test—a direct match to Marcus Wallace. And the bills in the duffle bag were of the same series as the bills we found in Marcus' pockets when he died. We believe this money may have been the reason Marcus and Osiris beefed a while back."

"You think Osiris would kill Marcus himself?" I ask. "Not even hire someone?"

"Osiris was down and out. He needed cash. He couldn't afford to put a hit out. He tried to collect on the money himself. Marcus wasn't giving it up, so he shot him, hopped a cab, and left the cash in his hobo sack in the trunk."

"But Osiris would never leave cash behind."

"I think something shook him, maybe he saw some cops and didn't want to risk the trouble if they recognized him. Not that all this matters anyway. We've closed the case."

It's hard to digest. The money Dooney gave me stained with Marcus' blood, left in a cab along with my clothes and Marcus' phone number. The hedge has been removed and the floodgates are open. I'm doing what Job was too afraid to do. I'm cursing God. I'm cursing this city. Is there not one good person left? Or do the good ones die or end up victims like Tammy? I thought Marcus was like a son to Dooney. I thought I was like a son to him. But now I see, maybe he just treated us like the bastards we were. Was he just trying to get rid of the bloody bills? He knew I was too down and out to question where the cash came from. I had assumed it was legit. But in this city who just gives a man a wad of cash for the hell of it? I've been a sucker, a new kind of fool. I thought Dooney was a guardian looking out for me. But maybe he's some kind of fraudulent angel, a serpent in disguise. I can conceive of death, but I can't conceive of betrayal. I'd rather have death than know Dooney too has betrayed me.

"I can have a patrol car take you to wherever you need to go," Moiye says.

"It's fine. I'll walk."

"Well, let me escort you out. It's better that way."

"Fine."

I follow Moiye out of the hot box and down the hallway of cops staring and whispering to each other.

"Don't mind them," Moiye says.

"I'm not. I know what they think of me. They're looking at me like I'm some kind of monster."

"You're not a monster."

"Then what am I?"

"You're a fool if you don't leave town. Remember what I told you about chances. As long as you're breathing, you've got a chance. This time don't waste it. Get out of town. Leave tonight. I've only got a few bucks, but it's something." He reaches into his pocket.

"Don't."

"It's not a problem, really."

"No, you don't understand," I say. "Tonight it ends. I'm not leaving this city. I'm not running anymore."

"You're talking crazy. Don't go and do something stupid."

"For what it's worth I probably wouldn't have made it this far without you, Moiye."

I begin to walk away, leaving Moiye in the hallway. He shouts to me: "Don't do anything stupid!"

It's too late. There is nothing Moiye or anyone else can say to convince me otherwise. I'm going to Dooney's. I'm going to confront him and I want him to look me in the eye and tell me he didn't have a hand in this. I want him to tell me he didn't push bloody bills on me, that he didn't kill Marcus and send Osiris to Tammy's doorstep.

I exit the station and despite the urge I have to smoke a cigarette, this time I don't stop to bum one from the cops on the precinct steps. I'm on a mission. I've got a meeting with the king of deceit. If I have to I'll spend all night tracking him down—a livid bloodhound, I'll sniff him out, following his trail of lies. I will shake him loose of this city. It won't be hard. If Dooney isn't at the barbershop, he's at home or maybe over at Morton's Jazz Café if he's feeling good.

I take a cab toward the barbershop and have it drop me off about a block away near the alley where I was accosted by the businessman. I survey the concrete and brick, taking slow and deliberate steps like a detective looking for clues at the scene of a crime. For me the alley is holy ground, a monument to all my follies. It's where I sealed my fate; taking that money from the businessman was a death sentence and now I'm almost done serving it. The hour is near, dead man walking. I guess I didn't have to be in prison to get on death row. I didn't even need a judge to sentence me. In the end I sentenced myself.

I've never really left prison. I tried to blame Tammy, believing my life with her was my prison, but that wasn't fair. I know now that the prison I was in was a prison of my own design. A prison built on the foundation of guilt, regret, hate, and anger. I hate who I am. I hate what I've done and that didn't go away the day I was released—all it did was get buried until it couldn't stay hidden any longer. And every time I looked at Tammy I was reminded how I didn't deserve her, how I didn't deserve any woman's love. Tammy was perfect and I found myself hating her for that. She reflected back on me all the ugliness that overcame me, dominated me, and enticed me to get behind the wheel drunk and strike down a little boy and his mother.

Rain begins to fall—drops hit the concrete sporadically as I head toward Dooney's barbershop. The neighborhood is dark. The city doesn't waste money bringing light to the ghetto. But the darkness is a comfort to me. Sometimes a man can see all he needs to in the dark. And as the rain mixes with old motor oil and garbage, the street turns slick.

My heartbeat feels like the countdown to something terrible, like the last few seconds on the clock ticking away until my final hour. If Dooney is a murderer, there's nothing stopping him from killing me. He's bigger, with brute strength. No matter what kind of fight I'd put up, Dooney could overpower me and though he may be even a greater monster than me, I don't know if I can raise a hand against him. Can a man raise his hand against someone he truly loves? They say men like me can't love. That everything we touch withers and dies because we've forgotten what it is to love or perhaps we've never known. Like animals, we breed, we fight, and we die. But to believe that is to believe there is a flaw in God's design—it's to believe that he made a mistake and populated animals with men, and it's the job of the men to keep us animals in line. Men like Moiye are there to keep beasts like me, Osiris, and Dooney at bay and to keep us away from the Tammys and Kims of the world.

In this society, the sanctified and the sinners are divided by race and wealth. But if I were to rip off my skin so that only my flesh and blood would be shown, would I get man's mercy then? If I was no longer a black man or an ex-convict, but a human being in the rawest of forms, consisting of only flesh, blood, organs, and veins, would they look at me as a poor soul? The result of some horrific accident, a burn victim, or perhaps a wounded soldier returned home from Iraq? Would I be pitied then?

But if so, first a sacrifice must be made, one that proves I'm worthy to be looked at as something more than what I am. I can be that sacrifice. I can make it so men like me won't be tested as Job was, so they can have a moment to breathe, a moment to feel apart of humanity again. So they can know what it's like to exist without the scarring of their past constantly flaring. Job was a pious man, a devout man, and he was treated like a dog. I am a dog and I will make the necessary sacrifice to be treated as a man, and if not in this life then perhaps God will see it fit in the next.

As I get closer to the shop I notice the light shining through the windows. It's the only light for miles on the dark stretch. I can feel the temperature in the air drop, turning cool and crisp. Has death arrived?

I push against the shop door slowly, and the bells that are

attached by string and nail chime.

"Hello?" Dooney calls out.

I remain silent.

"Who is it?" he asks. "Who's there?"

"It's me. Paul."

"Youngblood?"

Dooney steps out from a small office in the back of the shop.

"I get you at a bad time?" I ask.

"No, just going over this month's profits."

"How are things looking?"

"Ah, you don't want to hear about a broke man's troubles. I'm more interested in what you're still doing here in the city. I thought you would be long gone by now."

"I had a few last-minute things to tie up," I say. "I'm just about through. I'll be on my way soon."

"That right?" Dooney asks, focusing more on the view of the empty street than my words.

"Is something on your mind, Dooney?"

"I was thinking about getting a bite to eat," he says. "You feel like taking a ride with me?"

"Maybe," I say. "Where are you thinking about heading?"

"An Italian bistro," he says. "I've got a hankering for cold cuts."

"All right," I say, following Dooney out of the door. He takes a moment to lock up, pulling the accordion gate across the shop front and double-checking the lock.

The walk to the car is silent. Dooney shuffles about, keeping a slight distance ahead of me. I'm beginning to see him in a new light, as something ugly. I fight the urge to condemn him before I'm certain of the truth, but I can't help but feel I'm in the company of a cold-blooded killer.

Dooney quickly unlocks his car door and gets in. I get

in on the passenger side. He starts the engine and we drive toward South Street. Dooney is letting his foot do all the talking. We speed down a narrow one-way street, barely slowing at stop signs and for pedestrians.

"You must be pretty hungry," I say, jokingly.

Dooney doesn't laugh.

"This place has funny hours," he says. "I just don't want it to close on me."

"Must be some sandwich."

"Trust me. It's worth it."

We hit South Street and make a left. It isn't as busy as I expected. The rain must be keeping people inside tonight. Most of the time people scurry about, shopping, eating, and otherwise enjoying the summer nights, but tonight there's emptiness and danger in the air. Even the city feels it. It's telling people to stay in, that there's trouble cooking.

"Tell me something, Dooney."

"What do you wanna know?"

"When you were locked up, the first time, it was for killing a man, right?"

"That's right," he says.

"How did it happen?"

"It was a long time ago, kid. The details get fuzzy."

Dooney slams on the brakes for a group of boys on bikes riding against the green. The car screeches to an abrupt stop.

"Shit!" he shouts.

"Damn kids," I say.

Dooney composes himself, taking a deep breath and adjusting himself in the seat.

He takes a moment and then asks, "Why are you asking me this?"

"After I killed that mother and her boy, I was never the same. It wakes me up in the morning and puts me to bed at night. I live with it every second of my life."

"Well, it's something I choose not to remember," he says, driving at a slow pace, focusing hard on the street.

"But it's different for you, isn't it?" I ask. "You killed a man on purpose. I mean, it wasn't an accident—you weren't drunk or doped up."

"I did what I had to do to protect myself," he answers sharply.

"And if you had to, would you do it again?"

Dooney answers coldly, "In a heartbeat."

"I understand," I say.

"What is it, Paul? What are you trying to get at?"

"It's about Marcus. I need to know the truth about his death."

"Marcus? What the hell does that have to do with you?"

"I think you know, Dooney," I say.

Dooney makes a sharp right and heads down a small alley toward Front Street. He slows the car, rolling till a complete stop at the end of the alley.

"Where are we now?" I ask.

"You want to know about Marcus, don't you?" he says. "I'm going to show you."

Dooney locks the doors and speeds up, this time flying through stop signs as if they were nonexistent.

"I knew this was coming. I just knew you would look a gift horse in the mouth. You should have left town, Paul. You should have gotten out when you had a chance."

"What are you talking about?"

Dooney pulls up to a small lookout point on Front Street that faces the harbor.

"I gave you that money so you would get out and get on with your life. But you just had to stick around."

"Tell me about Jasmine, Dooney," I say. "She tracked me

down. She said she was pregnant with Marcus' baby."

"That son-of-a-bitch couldn't keep it in his pants," he says. "He had to sleep with everything that moved."

"Is that why he died?" I ask. "Did he and Jasmine really pocket the cash from the businessman job so they could get out of town with the baby?"

"It should have worked. All you had to do was show up. But you just had to pawn that job off on him." His tone is now one of resentment.

"You tried to bury it, didn't you?" I say. "Making people think Osiris had his hand in it, all while saving face in the shop. It was you, Dooney. You put Osiris' name in the mix, made a few calls to the precinct, an anonymous tip maybe. You made sure the streets were buzzing."

"And so what if I did? Marcus came by and picked me up from the shop. He was excited, flapping his gums about how he snatched that money and how he was going to run off with that drugged-up whore. He was going to walk out on his responsibilities, again. I couldn't let that happen to Shaina. She was better off without him."

"But Marcus wasn't sure it was his. He may have been a fool, but he knew his math. The months didn't add up. Marcus had broken it off with her when he supposedly got her pregnant. Isn't that what he confronted you about? It isn't Marcus' baby. It's yours."

"That's bullshit!"

"It's how you knew Shaina's house so well. It's why you were headed over there that day and it's why you jacked that money from Marcus. Marcus put it together, probably told you he would let everyone know the type of guy you were, creeping behind your own friend's back. Not even the ex-cons in the shop would cut you slack after Marcus ran his mouth on you for a bit. You wanted Marcus out of the picture and with the cash, your money troubles at the shop would fade. So you shot him, jacked him, and then pushed some of the bills on me, hoping the evidence would disappear when I did. But why me, Dooney?"

"Running his mouth was all Marcus was good at. I told him one day that mouth was going to get him killed. All I did was protect the life I made, my reputation, and my business. And as you know, reputation is all we got in these streets. Youngblood, you're nothing special out here. You had a woman, a life, and you were the fool who walked out on it. Why you? Because you didn't give a damn in the first place."

"You ruined lives," I say. "You ruined Tammy. Osiris called the shop and you gave her up."

"I wasn't interested in a beef with Osiris. I gave him what he wanted. I'm sorry Tammy had to lose in this, but that's as much your fault as it is mine."

"Yeah, but I didn't kill anybody."

"I did it for the right reasons."

"And now your child isn't going to have a father once the cops figure things out," I say.

"They aren't going to figure anything out if they haven't already," he says. "Osiris and Marcus are both six feet underground. The cops say the case is closed. It's over. Let it die. It's got nothing to do with you anyway."

"You're wrong, Dooney. It's got everything to do with me. Osiris went after Tammy over this mess and now she'll never be the same. But your blood money holds a secret. It's evidence, a smear of Marcus' blood on a bill. I suppose you forgot to check his pockets, even had a few bills on him when he died. And now it's in the hands of the city's best detective. He already knows about your shop and it'll only take me telling him the truth about you and Marcus for him to piece it all together."

"What the hell are you talking about? You telling me you turned that money in?"

Dooney tenses up and starts to shift in his seat, throwing his weight against the door and giving me a dead stare.

"Not me," I say. "But an honest man, maybe the last honest man in the city."

"You're lying."

"No, I'm not. I'm sorry, Dooney, but I just can't let this go."

Dooney pulls a small caliber piece from his back pocket, a pearl handle twenty-two.

"That's too damn bad," he says.

I think about Marcus. What was he feeling in this moment? Face-to-face with a man he called friend, a man who was prepared to kill him?

"I guess we all have it coming sooner or later," I say.

Everything falls silent. There isn't time to get out of the car. I hear the bang. I feel the heat and inhale the gun powder. The first shot burns beyond belief. The odor of scorched flesh fills the cabin. I breathe and the bullet shifts below my ribs. I scream.

It was suicide to confront Dooney like this. Or maybe I was asking for it. Maybe this is how I want it all to end. At least it's at the hands of a man I know, not some stranger or stick-up kid. Not that it matters. Death is death, but I'm relieved that it's Dooney.

The second shot pierces my shoulder. It feels more like a flesh wound but the impact sends me against the window, shattering the glass. I don't black out or go into shock. I look to Dooney, who has tears in his eyes, his arthritic hand barely able to hold the gun. Maybe it's the hand shakes that kept him from sending a bullet directly into my heart. Or maybe I'm destined to live through this. Either way, I can't let it claim me so easy, not tonight. Tonight, death has got to earn it.

I reach for the gun, keeping it low and pointed toward the floorboard. I force off more shots, pressing his finger against the trigger until the gun is nearly empty. His arms are tight and strong. Arthritis hasn't inflicted them. They're rippled with muscle and a force to be reckoned with. We struggle, the gun constantly being pointed in different directions, blood, sweat, and tears on the handle, in our palms and on our shirts. It's intimate and brutal, like being born. Dooney lets out a grunt and the final shot rings. Dooney stops struggling and I realize he's been hit. The bullet is lodged in his chest. His jaw drops and he trembles. The red begins to run thick and fast. I knock the gun away, sending it to the floor. I take Dooney by the hand and hold it tight. I know he wouldn't have done the same for me, but for some reason I'm compelled. My friend is going home.

"Paul? Paul?" His voice is scratchy, and blood bubbles in the corners of his mouth and collects at the base of his nose.

"Go home, Dooney. Go home."

I wait until his breathing gets shallow. It goes from heavy to a hum and then to a whimper, and a final sigh. I place his hand in his lap and brush his eyelids closed.

Dooney is dead.

"Goodbye," I say, as I recline in the seat and wait for death.

CHAPTER ELEVEN

DEATH DOESN'T COME. With every swallow I can taste the gunpowder in my throat. I bleed long enough to lose consciousness. When I come to, a flashlight is shining in my eyes, and I can smell freshly liquored breath.

"Hey, boy, wake up!" a voice shouts.

I look over to Dooney, whose head is slumped down chin to chest. If I didn't know better, I'd swear he was asleep. Sometimes it's hard to tell the living from the dead.

The call goes out: "I've got two gun-shot victims. Possible D.O.As," the voice says.

I realize the officers think I'm dead. I struggle to move my arms, but they've gone stiff. I take a deep breath and focus my efforts on unlocking the doors. I push the automatic lock and use my index finger to pull at the door handle. It takes minutes, but feels like an eternity before I get the door unlocked. I press against the door, propping my weight on the armrest until it swings open and I spill out. My face smacks against the wet pavement, blood like rainwater pouring from the holes in my body.

"Jesus Christ, we've got a live one," a voice says.

A hand takes a hold of my arm and forces me on my back. I can barely make out their faces, but I recognize their voices. It's the skinny and fat cop from the alley outside Tammy's brownstone, Wilson and his superior—the skinny cop's black sneakers confirm it.

"The one in the car is dead for sure," Wilson says. "We'll see if this one holds out long enough for the medics."

"Niggers and their guns," the fat cop says bluntly.

Niggers and their guns—the phrase seems to echo over and over in my mind. I should be disgusted by it, but for some reason the phrase makes sense and my heart gets heavy from the thought that blacks and violence are somehow synonymous. But in my life I haven't proven otherwise. I've watched my life and the lives of other black men crumble at the hands of violence. Even when I've had chances to stop it, I haven't. I successfully destroyed every good thing in my otherwise pathetic life and I did it to feed this unholy obsession with the streets and in turn the streets inflicted insurmountable pain on my body, mind, and soul.

I think about my grandfather and wonder what he would say if he could see me lying in a puddle, bleeding out while two racist cops drink and smoke cigarettes waiting for an ambulance to come and save my life. Whether I live or die, depending on how fast that ambulance can arrive. I suppose he would say it was my own doing. That the decisions I've made were sure to have me in this situation, or perhaps he would just offer his pity.

I can feel my body shutting down. The world around me seems like the volume is being lowered, like a stage curtain closing on the final act. I think about how Tammy would pray for me. I've never felt like those prayers did much good. But maybe tonight those prayers will be answered, or maybe it's time for me to take a leap of faith. I haven't prayed for anything since I was a child. I don't even know how to begin. I think about God and the angels and heaven, but it all seems like something out of a storybook. So instead I call out to whatever is listening. I call out to a God I haven't spoken to in years or perhaps one I've never known. I ask him to save me. I promise him that I won't waste another chance. I beg him to spare me as he did Job, and I patiently await his answer.

CHAPTER TWELVE

THEY SHINE A SMALL PENLIGHT into my eyes and shove oxygen tubes into my nostrils. The nurse asks my name, but it's too painful to speak. My throat has gone dry from the oxygen. They wheel me down the hallway. The fluorescent lights are reminiscent of the hot boxes I spent hours in. They run an IV into my arm and then inject something that sends fire through my veins.

I think about black flesh and all the strange things that could be happening to it at this moment. Somewhere black flesh is being born, being bruised, being buried, sweating, loving, dreaming, and dying. Black bodies locked away in prison cells, starving, slaving, and weeping in the moonlight. I think of the infinite postures, smiles, and gestures. The countless black expressions, sayings, greetings, and goodbyes, and then with the little breath left in my body, I quietly laugh. I laugh for all the beauty, horrors, terrors, and despairs they could be suffering through at this moment. I laugh until tears stream down my face and the nurse blots them dry, reassuring me everything is going to be all right. I laugh, convinced it will be the last act I'll ever commit.

I'm dying and it's the closest connection to humanity I've ever had because in the end we all die, no matter what race or gender, no matter whether we're rich or poor, convict or cop. We all have to leave this earth one day and face whatever is after.

The hospital is loud and the walls are closing in on me. I've never missed the quiet of the farm as much as I do right now—the cemetery silence, as if time has stopped, and not even the tiny particles in the air dare brave the slightest of movements. But here, noise consumes everything: the chattering voices, the rolling of wheelchairs, the barrage of footsteps, the tender cries, the whispered prayers. I imagine life in the city outside of the hospital—traveling the streets as a specter, looking into the windows of the unsuspecting. Watching as a family enjoys dinner at the table, a couple in the midst of a welcome home embrace, a college student cramming for a test, and an old man falling asleep to the evening news.

They wheel me into an operating room and place me on a cold table. The surgeon counts down from ten to one. The injection takes effect and an ominous darkness falls upon the room, and in seconds everything ceases to be.

I feel the life get pushed back inside me. It feels like a hot dagger to my heart and I awaken to the nurses and the surgeon hovering over me.

"Paul, can you hear me?" the surgeon asks, holding shock panels.

"Wake up for us, Paul," the nurse says.

I force my eyes open despite the soreness of the bright lights.

"He's back," the nurse says. "Let's get him to recovery."

They wheel me out of the operating room and down the hall to another room. It's the cleanest room I've ever been in. It smells of bleach and rubbing alcohol. There's a large three-pane window that overlooks the city, and the moon is full, shining through the glass. It's a beautiful night, but it's hell inside these walls.

The nurses lift and slide me from the stretcher to the bed. They connect the pulse monitor to my middle finger and reconnect the oxygen tubes. They attach my IV to a new fluid pack.

"We're giving you a pain button," she says. "It will give you a dose of morphine any time you need it. Just push this button." She holds up a small plastic button connected to a morphine drip.

I nod my head so she knows I understand and watch as the nurses leave. I push the morphine button and fall back asleep.

I awake to the morning sun warm on my skin. A tall nurse with brown and blonde-streaked hair and a vacation tan comes in with the surgeon, a white man with blue eyes and a hawk-nose profile. He introduces himself as Dr. Schuster and adjusts the mini-blinds so the sunlight isn't blinding me. He holds a chart; a ballpoint pen is lodged between his fingers. The nurse puts a thick brown shake in my face and tells me to drink. I take a few sips, and then she sets it on the tray in front of me. Schuster explains that he was able to remove the bullet from my shoulder, but a fragment of the bullet remains in my chest. He tells me I'm lucky the bullet didn't hit any organs or major arteries, but there is still a chance the bullet will shift and cause damage later. I mutter a few words that make sense in my head, but I'm unsure of what comes out of my mouth. The nurse encourages me to drink some more of the chalky concoction, but I refuse. Schuster announces he has more patients to see and they leave. I press the morphine button.

When I awake, night has fallen and my chest wound is bleeding. I hit the nurses' call button. A petite woman with light brown skin, Asian, maybe Pinoy, enters dressed in pink-and-white-flowered scrubs. She cleans the wound and changes the dressing. She tries to make small talk, but gives up after a few minutes of my nods and grunts. Even if I could formulate words, I can't imagine I'd have anything to say to her outside of answering her questions about how I'm feeling.

The nurse takes a seat and turns on the television. I don't know if she's doing it as a courtesy or just taking advantage of a speechless patient. She flips channels, mumbling to herself. She finally settles on an evening sitcom. Her laughter nearly drowns out the sound of Moiye coming through the door holding a brown paper bag and newspaper. The nurse gets nervous and quickly turns off the television. Moiye flashes his badge and she scurries out of the room, shutting the door behind her. He sets the paper bag down on the floor and opens the folded newspaper to the front page. He's weathered, and his green eyes look sleepy and heavy.

"They say you can't talk, but I assume you can listen."

He holds up the front page for me to see. Two men dressed in blue nylon jackets with F.B.I. in gold letters on their backs are escorting the businessman, Mr. Washington, out of a lavish high-rise in cuffs. Moiye begins to read. I listen intently. By the time he reaches the end of the article, I want to speak. I want to tell him everything I know, how I shot Dooney in self-defense, but just the thought of speaking makes me ill. My throat is caked with dried blood and mucus, and every time I cough I send crusted blood and yellow fluid onto my nightgown.

"Harlin Washington was paying off city workers to forge inspection documents stating his buildings were up-to-code. Meanwhile folks were falling through the second floors. This is the biggest illegal operation involving city workers in decades. It'll take the city years to recover from it. The name of your recently deceased friend, Dooney, has come up quite a bit in his statements and Mr. Washington is claiming he hired a mysterious fella from the barbershop to do some work for him. He's naming every felon he can in order to get a lighter sentence and one of the descriptions he gave sounds a lot like you. Now I can try and keep you from going down for Dooney, but Washington is the feds business. You get implicated in that and you're on your own."

I can't believe Moiye is here bailing me out again. I signal to him for a writing pen and paper. He slides his pad over to me with a black ballpoint with a gold cap. I write IT WAS SELF-DEFENSE.

"Maybe so, but it won't matter if they connect you to this city worker sting. With Harlin Washington talking, he could easily get you caught up in this mess if someone gets wise enough to show him your photo. And the way his lawyer is working it, he's demanding surveillance photos of every ex-con that's ever set foot in that barbershop. As far as Dooney, no one has even come to identify his body. He's being housed at the morgue pending autopsy. Right now, you're just a person of interest."

I'm not surprised Shaina hasn't shown to ID Dooney. I'm sure losing two men in your life back-to-back would make any woman turn into a shut-in. I wonder if Dooney really loved Shaina and if she really loved him. Or was her love only as deep as Dooney's pockets and Dooney's love only as genuine as the late-nights when the wine was flowing and

Marcus was away. Shaina's unborn child is the embodiment of two grown folks' mistake. Without a father and Shaina as a mother, that child's life is already in peril. It needs a Messiah, they all do, someone who can come and wrap the entire city's young in loving arms and carry them off to a better place so they don't grow up and become like Marcus, Jasmine, Osiris, Dooney, or even me.

I write on the pad WHO'S HEADING THE INVESTIGATION?

Moiye smiles awkwardly and says, "Probably two wet-behind-the-ears detectives. Tomorrow morning the autopsy will be complete and if the evidence supports your self-defense claim, they'll close the case. But if it doesn't, there isn't much I'll be able to do for you. You have thirteen hours to get out of town and manage not to bleed to death doing it. I brought you some things from the precinct's unclaimed property." He picks the brown bag up from the floor and sets it at the end of the bed.

My body may be broken, but my thoughts are intact and they've never been clearer. Moiye has been the closest thing I have to a friend in these past few sobering days.

"By the way, I'll be checking on Tammy, making sure she's getting along all right," he says, folding his newspaper and tucking it under his arm.

Moiye actually cares about what happens to me and Tammy. I don't know why. I'm just happy he does. I'm happy someone does.

I try to hand him his pen and pad, but he tells me to keep it and then somberly walks out of the room. I don't know if Moiye thinks I'm innocent or guilty in Dooney's death, or if it matters to him. I wonder if he doubts I'll even live long enough to face a trial—that I'll most likely die on the run—enjoying a few hours of freedom before being found slumped over in some bus station. I've been near death plenty of times, once after contracting meningitis as a boy, later in a prison riot, and then, a near-victim of a mean drunk with a sharp blade. I don't doubt that I'll live. I'm just concerned with the type of life I'll have.

This is my only chance at freedom and I have to take it. I can't place my fate in the hands of the Philadelphia Police Department. Evidence could be botched. They could find me guilty of murder and not self-defense, simply because black-on-black crime isn't worth investigating thoroughly. It's happened before: countless brothers locked up for crimes they were innocent of. I trust Moiye, but not the department, not enough to stay in town while the investigation is under-way. Young detectives are always eager to garnish a reputa-tion and I can't risk becoming a bull's prize collar.

This was Moiye's farewell and final helping hand. He's leaving me with a seed of hope. If I make it out of Philly, I have a chance, or I can stay till morning and face the possi-bility of having to return to prison. With my history and a state-appointed attorney, I could easily be put away by a jury of my so-called peers, and I wouldn't last a day behind bars.

By now, news of Dooney's death is circulating the prison yards. The hour I'd show up to serve, I'd be marked for a hit. I'm a dead man in or out of prison. The longer I stay in this city the more dangerous things will get. Dooney had friends, and even though he was a killer, he did more for ex-cons than the city ever did. He cared when the city just turned its back. The right ex-con wouldn't hesitate to end my life in some misguided act of revenge.

I check my wounds to ensure they're not bleeding and remove the oxygen from my nose, along with the IV from my arm and the pulse monitor from my finger, which beeps incessantly until I unplug the cord. It takes me twenty minutes to get out of bed. When I do I'm light-headed and nearly vomit. I rummage through the brown bag Moiye left. It's full of abandoned clothes that stink of piss and cigarette smoke.

I remove a pair of sweatpants, a T-shirt that reads Drexel University, and a pair of flip-flops from the bag. While putting on the clothes, I nearly topple over twice from a sharp pain in my chest. I try to move quickly, fearing the nurse will return any minute and foil my escape.

I work my legs into the sweatpants that look as if they were left behind by a much larger man. The drawstring is stretched and the pants hang baggy around my waist. I'm unable to put the shirt on completely due to the sling on my arm, and I let the right sleeve rest on my shoulder. I slide my feet into the flip-flops and shuffle across the linoleum to the door.

I look through the rectangle of tempered glass and struggle to see as far down the hallway as I can. It's late, and I imagine only two nurses to be on duty, one sitting at the desk and the other making rounds. A nurse normally comes in to check on me every thirty minutes give or take, which gives me about ten minutes to get down to the lobby.

I open the door slowly, looking left and then right. The elevator is about twenty paces away. My legs are weak and my knees are just short of buckling. My face feels swollen and tight. I can still taste the gunpowder in the back of my throat and my stitches are already beginning to itch. I probably look like the walking dead. The floor is silent. I can hear the pulse monitors beep in other patients' rooms and the phone ringing in the nurse's station. I think I can make it to the elevator without being noticed and hit the button to go down. I try to keep focused and my mind from wandering. But all I can see is the nurse rounding the corner any minute and dragging me back to bed. She could easily be on the elevator returning from covering a lunch break in the upstairs cancer ward.

The elevator doors open, and I'm relieved it's just a member of the cleaning crew pushing a cart of freshly washed towels and linen. She's a short woman with curly black hair and a beauty mark above her lip. Her light blue name tag reads LOLA. She pauses a moment, not fully alarmed, but somewhat concerned as she looks at my condition.

"Sir, where are you going?" she asks in a thick European accent.

"Everything . . . is . . . fine," I say.

My words are coarse and broken. My throat stings from letting so much air in to speak and I fall into a coughing fit.

I regret saying anything. If everything is fine, there's no reason to announce it. All I did was let her know that something was wrong. If I had been discharged, I'd be leaving in a wheelchair with at least one accompanying nurse. It doesn't take a medical degree to know my bandages are covering fresh wounds.

Lola pushes the cart past me and quickly heads for the nurses' station. I walk into the elevator and press the button for the lobby. I curse my weak legs and not being able to take the stairs. There wouldn't be much foot traffic at this hour. But there's no point in wishing for the impossible. I just need to make it out of the lobby without being hassled.

I reach the lobby floor and I'm greeted by waiting patients: crying babies, an elderly man hooked to an oxygen tank, a young boy with a broken arm, everyone in too much pain to pay me any mind. I shuffle toward the sliding doors. Medics rush past me wheeling in another gunshot victim. I'm back with humanity. I've been given another chance and this time I have to make it work. David Hume believed the life of a man is no more consequential than that of an oyster, but I can't believe that. I can't afford to believe that. I have to believe as I did in prison, that one day, somehow, my situation can and will improve, because I'm meant for more. My destiny isn't to die on these streets; it's to live, to thrive, and to find happiness. And I'm willing to fight for that happiness—I'm willing to die for it.

There is a remedy, a way to exist in this world and I will find it. I've stepped out of darkness, and for now, I'm only living by my grandfather's words: "Nobody said living would be easy, but someone had to do it."

I walk out of the hospital and into the night. The city is loud. The volume has been turned back up, but louder than before. Police sirens and car horns and curses and shouts—a symphony of chaos. I head toward Broad Street, tired, in pain and penniless, but not without hope. As long as I'm breathing I've still got a chance. All I need is a light to see my way.

AARON PHILIP CLARK is a novelist and screenwriter from Los Angeles, CA. His work has been praised by James Sallis, Gar Anthony Haywood, Gary Phillips, Eric Beetner, and Roger Smith. In addition to his writing career, he has worked in the film industry and law enforcement. Clark currently teaches English and writing courses at a university in Southern California.

To learn more about him, please visit AaronPhilipClark.com.

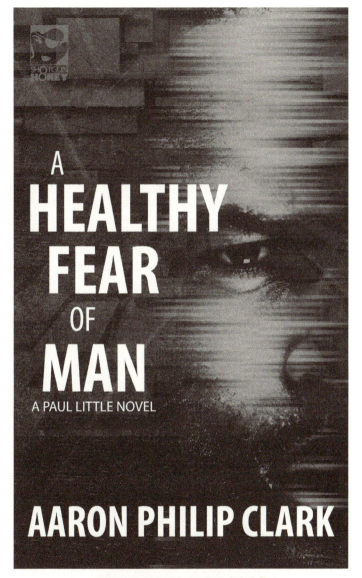

A

HEALTHY
FEAR
OF
MAN

A PAUL LITTLE NOVEL

AARON PHILIP CLARK

AVAILABLE JUNE 2018
ONLY FROM SHOTGUN HONEY

On the following pages are a few
more great titles from the
Down & Out Books publishing family.

For a complete list of books and to
sign up for our newsletter,
go to **DownAndOutBooks.com**.

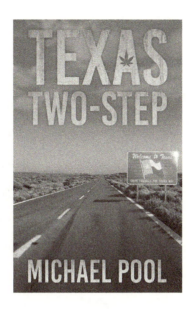

Texas Two-Step
A Russ Kirkpatrick Novel
Michael Pool

Down & Out Books
April 2018
978-1-946502-56-8

Cooper and Davis are a couple of Widespread Panic-obsessed Texas ex-pats growing some of Denver's finest organic cannabis. At least they were, until legal weed put the squeeze on their market. When their last out-of-state dealer gets busted, they're left with no choice but to turn to their reckless former associate Sancho Watts to unload one last crop in Teller County, Texas.

What ensues is an East Texas criminal jamboree with everyone involved keeping their cards so close to their vest that all the high-stakes dancing around each other is sure to result in bloodshed.

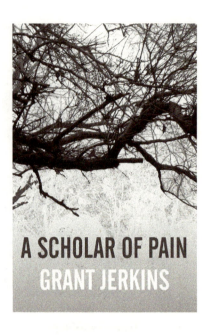

A Scholar of Pain
Grant Jerkins

ABC Group Documentation
an imprint of Down & Out Books
February 2018
978-1-946502-15-5

In his debut short fiction collection, Grant Jerkins remains—as the Washington Post put it—"Determined to peer into the darkness and tell us exactly what he sees." Here, the depth of that darkness is on evident, oftentimes poetic, display. Read all sixteen of these deviant diversions. Peer into the darkness.

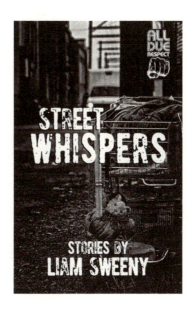

Street Whispers
Stories by Liam Sweeny

All Due Respect
an imprint of Down & Out Books
February 2018
978-1-946502-86-5

An eclectic collection of pulp, grit and noir stories inspired
by the Capital Region of New York, a rust-belt crossroads in
the shadow of the city that never sleeps.

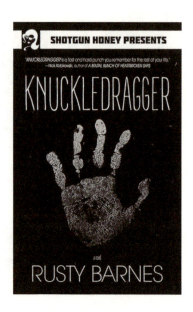

Knuckledragger
Rusty Barnes

Shotgun Honey
an imprint of Down & Out Books
October 2017
978-1-946502-07-0

Hooligan and low-level criminal enforcer Jason "Candy" Stahl has made a good life collecting money for his boss Otis. One collection trip, though, at the Diovisalvo Liquor Store, unravels events that turn Candy's life into a horror-show.

In quick succession he moves up a notch in the organization, overseeing a chop shop, while he falls in lust with Otis's girlfriend Nina, gets beaten for insubordination, and is forced to run when Otis finds out about Candy and Nina's affair.

WITHDRAWN
BY
WILLIAMSBURG REGIONAL LIBRARY

CPSIA information can be obtained
at www.ICGtesting.com
Printed in the USA
LVHW092040181118
597559LV00003BA/433/P

9 781948 235006